DARREN SHAN
ZOM-B
GLADIATOR

SIMON & SCHUSTER

First published in Great Britain in 2014 by Simon and Schuster UK Ltd
This edition published 2016
A CBS COMPANY

1 3 5 7 9 10 8 6 4 2

Simon & Schuster UK Ltd
1st Floor, 222 Gray's Inn Road
London WC1X 8HB

Simon & Schuster Australia, Sydney
Simon & Schuster India, New Delhi

A CIP catalogue copy for this book
is available from the British Library.

HB ISBN: 978-0-85707-772-1
PB ISBN: 978-1-4711-5835-3
EBOOK ISBN: 978-0-85707-775-2

Printed and bound by CPI Group (UK) Ltd, Croydon, CR0 4YY

MIX
Paper from
responsible sources
FSC® C020471

Simon & Schuster UK Ltd are committed to sourcing paper
that is made from wood grown in sustainable forests and support the Forest
Stewardship Council, the leading international forest certification organisation.
Our books displaying the FSC logo are printed on FSC certified paper.

www.simonandschuster.co.uk
www.simonandschuster.com.au

For:
my best men and ushers – thanks for
accompanying me into the deadliest arena
in the world!

OBE (Order of the Bloody Entrails) to:
"Lady" Jade Westwood

Gladiatorial mentors:
Venetia Gosling
Kate Sullivan

Arena impresarios: the Christopher Little Agency

THEN . . .

Zombies ripped Becky Smith's heart from her chest and turned her into an undead, brain-munching beast. But several months later she recovered her senses and became a revitalised, a rare member of the undead who could think and control her cannibalistic urges.

Death was far harder for B than life had ever been. First she was held prisoner in an underground complex with a pack of teenaged revitaliseds. With the exception of B and one other, Rage, they were all fried by soldiers with flame-throwers when a killer clown invaded the complex and started a riot.

B broke free of the underground lair and found a London she barely recognised. Zombies had taken over. The few humans she crossed paths with all seemed as vicious as their undead foes—a hunter called Barnes and his posse slaughtered zombies for fun, a rifle-packing group on HMS *Belfast* opened fire on anything that came within range, while the deranged clown and his mutant army spread terror and carnage wherever they set foot.

She finally found refuge in County Hall, a massive building behind the London Eye. A century-old zombie, Dr Oystein, had set up base there and was offering sanctuary to any revitalised who asked it of him. He had also recruited a few humans, such as Billy Burke, B's former teacher, and Reilly, a soldier and one of her captors in the underground complex.

Dr Oystein believed he was on a mission from God. He said that the clown B had encountered, the chilling and crazy Mr Dowling, worked for the Devil. If Dr Oystein and his zombie Angels didn't defeat Mr Dowling and his mutants, the last remaining survivors in the world would fall and Satan would claim their souls.

B thought the doctor was insane. Although she feared being alone, and was worried about what would happen next, she turned her back on County Hall and left to find somewhere else in the city to call home.

She ended up in the studio of Timothy Jackson, an artist who spent his days painting what he saw on the streets of zombie-infected London. Timothy took her to meet a strange baby which he had found. It was sexless and monstrous. A spike was sticking out of its head and it hadn't eaten in weeks, yet it was still somehow alive.

When B removed the spike, the baby screamed for help and dozens of zombies responded to its call. They flocked to the studio, broke in, killed Timothy and made off with the baby, but not before it had asked B to accompany them. It called her its mummy and said she was one of them.

B refused to go with the inhuman baby and its undead coterie. But her world was changed, as was her opinion of Dr Oystein and his claim to be in contact with God. Because B had dreamt of babies like this one when she was alive. In her dreams they had looked exactly like this child, behaved the same way, said the same things. And, despite her scepticism, B had to conclude that a higher power must have sent her the dreams as a warning, to prepare her for this day and provide her with the evidence she'd need in order to accept Dr Oystein's far-fetched claims.

B returned to County Hall, pledged herself to Dr Oystein then hopped into one of his body-reviving Groove Tubes to restore her sharpness and strength, so that she would be fresh and ready for the war with Mr Dowling which was to come.

NOW . . .

ONE

There's a tunnel beneath Waterloo Station that used to be a haven for graffiti artists. Anyone was allowed to paint whatever they wanted on the walls, floor or ceiling.

The zombies put a stop to the artists with their stencils and spray paint, but the art remains, bright, bold and colourful. It covers every inch of the tunnel. If humans ever eliminate the undead and take control of the world again, I bet a lot of people will come to this place to admire the paintings.

But I'm not here today for the graffiti.

I'm here for the zombies.

We usually keep this tunnel clear of the living dead. It's easily done. Zombies have sensitive ears. High-pitched noises cut through our skulls and make our teeth shake. When Dr Oystein moved into County Hall, he placed speakers in hidden places around the area and played a loop of sharp noises through them, guaranteed to send any zombie within range running for cover. It keeps the drooling, brain-hungry riff-raff from our door.

But we haven't been playing the loop in the tunnel for the last few nights. We wanted company and figured the dark, quiet space would draw a crowd once we cut the power to the speakers.

We figured right. There are twenty-five or thirty zombies in residence, a mix of men, women and kids, some in suits or nice dresses, others in more casual wear, a few naked or as good as. Blank expressions, long, sharp teeth, bones sticking out of their fingers and toes, wisps of green moss wherever they were bitten or cut when they were alive.

I study the zombies with a touch of nerves, but no

disgust, revulsion or pity. They're my own kind. Except for the fact that my brain works, I'm no different to them.

I'm part of a group of six. The others are the same as me, revitalised Angels, soldiers in Dr Oystein's undead army. Carl Clay stands to my left, looking impeccable in his top-of-the-range, designer gear. Ashtat Kiarostami is to my right, dressed in a blue, loose-fitting suit, with a white headscarf. The bulky Rage is on the other side of Carl, wearing the leathers that he's favoured since his time as a zom head. Shane Fitz and Jakob Pegg are next to Ashtat, Shane looking as yobbish as ever in a tracksuit and with a gold chain dangling from his neck, Jakob pale and sickly in a pair of jeans and a shirt that sags on his bony frame.

We're all unarmed.

'Do you think there are enough of them?' Carl asks, frowning as he counts the zombies.

'Five to one,' Shane sniffs. 'Those are long enough odds for me. How many more do you want to face?'

'There aren't many men among them,' Carl notes.

'Are you suggesting that women are inferior?' Ashtat asks coldly.

Carl winces. 'No. But generally speaking they're not as strong as men. It's the way of the world. You can't argue with that.'

'In life, no,' Ashtat says. 'But death levels the playing field. I have noticed no real difference between the sexes in our battles so far. Muscles are not the factor they once were, not in reviveds. Or revitaliseds,' she adds pointedly.

Carl makes a sighing sound, which isn't easy when you don't have functioning lungs. 'All right. I don't want an argument. Are we all happy to press ahead? We don't want to wait another day in case more of them come to seek shelter here?' He looks around and everyone shrugs or nods. 'Fair enough. We'll crack on. How about you, Reilly? Are you ready?'

The soldier is standing behind us. He's not a happy bunny.

'I can't believe I let Zhang talk me into this,' he mutters. He's sweating. That's something no revitalised could ever mimic. The walking dead don't sweat.

12

'Don't be a baby,' Rage grins. 'We've all got to be prepared to make sacrifices for the cause.'

'Yeah?' Reilly snarls. 'What have *you* sacrificed lately?'

'My sense of compassion,' Rage snaps. 'Now quit moaning or we'll leave you here by yourself. Are you ready or not?'

'I suppose,' Reilly mutters miserably. He's really not enjoying this. I don't blame him. It can't be easy, placing your life in the hands of a surly shower of teenage zombies.

Ashtat and I nudge apart and Reilly steps through the gap. He's covered himself from the neck down in thick leathers and he's wearing a helmet with a tough glass visor. The gear won't protect him for long if a zombie gets hold of him and rips in, but it should guard him against casual swipes, spit and flying blood.

Reilly moves a couple of metres ahead of us, gulps, then calls out loudly, 'I don't suppose any of you creeps have seen Banksy?'

The zombies didn't pay much attention to us when

we filed in. They could tell from our moss-covered wounds and the bones jutting out of our fingertips that we were in the same boat as them.

Reilly is a whole different kettle of fish. When he shouts, they jerk to attention and lock their sights on him. They note his covered form, his shaky grin behind the visor. They clock his heartbeat. They smell his blood, fresh and pure, his sweat, the scent of the food he ate that morning on his lips and tongue, his juicy brain.

The zombies howl with glee and hunger, a penetrating, fearsome sound. Then they move as one and surge towards us, fingers flexing, teeth gnashing, primed, deadly assassins whose only purpose in this world is to attack and tear asunder.

It's killing time!

TWO

We dart ahead of Reilly and tackle the onrushing zombies. I run into a woman who is wearing a bra and knickers and nothing else. There are curlers in her hair. Looks like the living dead caught her at home when she was getting ready to go out.

I strike swiftly at the woman, a flurry of blows to her face and neck. She snarls and tries to hit back. I turn quickly, raising my leg high, and kick the back of her head as I spin. She's slammed sideways. I'm on her instantly. Making the fingers of my right hand straight and hard, I drive the bones sticking out of them down sharply into her skull, piercing the covering of bone, digging into the vulnerable brain beneath.

The woman shudders, makes a low moaning noise, then falls still. I withdraw my hand and leave her to lie in the dust of the tunnel, truly dead now.

A man is rushing past me, hands outstretched, reaching for Reilly. I elbow him in the ribs. I can't knock the wind out of his sails – there's no wind in them to begin with – but the force of the blow sends him off course. As he staggers, I follow after him, fingers ready to crack open another head and rid the city of one more zombie.

I don't like doing this. I refused to kill reviveds when I was a prisoner in the military complex. But Dr Oystein has convinced me that it's necessary. If we are to triumph in the war to come, we need to sharpen ourselves in combat. So, as much as I hate it, I kill as ordered, but I do it quickly and cleanly, not wanting to torment these poor lost souls.

The other Angels are busy around me. Each of us has a different ability and we've all been trained by

Master Zhang to focus on our strengths. We've been told to test specific skills today, to only deviate from them if absolutely necessary. Mine is the speed with which I can strike—I have quick hands and feet, very nimble.

Ashtat is our pack's version of the Karate Kid. She whirls gracefully around the tunnel, chopping and kicking, leaping high into the air to casually swing a foot at a man's head—a second later it's been knocked clear of his neck. She lands smoothly, pounces after the head, comes down on it with a well-placed heel to squish the brain and put the zombie out of action.

Rage is a one-man wrecking machine. He's the strongest of us all. He lets his opponents get close, then clubs them over the head or grabs them in a bear hug and squeezes until their brains seep out through their eye sockets and ear canals. He laughs and cracks jokes as he kills. He doesn't have any of the reservations that I do.

Posh Carl can jump like a grasshopper. He leaps around, landing among the reviveds, disrupting and

scattering them, pushing them over or tripping them up, then springing across the tunnel to strike again. He could kill easily but he's been told not to. Today he's just here to confuse and disrupt.

Jakob isn't killing either. He's under orders to protect Reilly from any revived that gets past the rest of us. Jakob can run very fast. He's skinny and unhealthy-looking, even for a zombie, the result of the cancer he was dying from when he was turned. He's always in pain, but he can shrug it off when he has to. In the tunnel he stays focused, pulling Reilly away from stray zombies, ready to pick him up and run with him if something goes seriously wrong and the rest of us get into difficulties.

Ginger Shane's fingerbones and toe bones are tougher than anyone else's. We can all dig our bones into planks or crumbling bricks, but Shane can gouge a hole in a slab of concrete. He keeps climbing the walls and dropping on our opponents. He's laughing like Rage – the pair have become thick as thieves – until one of the zombies snags the gold chain around his neck and rips it loose.

'Not my chain!' Shane roars as it flies across the tunnel. He loses interest in the zombie and hurries after the keepsake.

'Shane!' Ashtat snaps. 'Don't abandon your position.'

'Get stuffed,' he grunts, shoving a zombie out of his way, scooping to reclaim his cherished possession.

A female zombie attacks him from the side as he's brushing dirt from the chain. He goes down with a cry of surprise. The woman tears at him, digs her fingers into his stomach, bites down hard on his left shoulder.

Shane roars and slaps the revived. He shouts for help. Ashtat curses and starts towards him, but Jakob is faster. Forgetting his orders, he abandons Reilly and races to the aid of his friend, tugging the zombie away, buying Shane time to get back on his feet.

'Where's my bloody guard gone?' Reilly bellows. Then, a second later, he moans, 'Oh crap.'

A couple of zombies have broken through and are bearing down on him. Reilly turns to run but the living dead are faster. One, a guy, grabs his waist. The other, a woman, tries to chew through his helmet.

For a second I freeze, imagining having to break Reilly's loss to Ciara, the always stylishly dressed dinner lady who fixes our meals at County Hall. The pair of living humans have recently started dating, after the shy Reilly finally worked up the courage to ask her out. He didn't tell her he was coming with us today. Didn't want her to worry.

Snapping back into action, I throw myself in Reilly's direction, praying I'm not too late. But Carl beats me to the punch. He leaps in out of nowhere, kicks the head of the woman chewing on Reilly's helmet, grabs the ears of her partner and tugs sharply. Zombies don't feel pain as much as the living, but we can be hurt. The man screeches and loses interest in Reilly. He bats Carl away, then dives after him.

The woman is back at Reilly's helmet again, but before she can bare her fangs and chow down, Ashtat is on her, kicking furiously, short, sharp jabs, forcing her to retreat.

I attack the undead man from behind. I thrust a

hand into his back and out through his chest. His heart bursts and chunks drip from my fingers. That won't stop him – zombies can survive without any organ except their brain – but it sure as hell distracts him. He writhes like a speared fish, trying to tear free.

I hold firm, wrapping my other arm round him, jamming my face in close to his back to present less of a target for his flailing arms. As he struggles, Carl makes a blade of his fingers, takes aim, then sends his left hand shooting through the revived's right eye. He goes in up to his wrist, then sneers at the zombie as he stiffens and dies.

'That'll teach you to mess with the Clay.'

'Are you all right?' I shout at Reilly. He's patting himself, checking for rips in his leathers, features twisted frantically behind the visor. 'Reilly! Are you OK?'

'I think so,' he wheezes, starting to relax. 'I don't think I've been scratched. Where the hell is Jakob?'

'Helping Shane.'

Reilly growls. 'My boot's gonna be helping its

way up his arse when I get him back to County Hall.'

'No swearing,' Rage crows as he grabs the head of a boy who can't be more than eight or nine years old. 'You'll set a bad example.'

'A lot of use you were,' I throw back at him.

Rage shrugs. 'Doesn't matter to me if Reilly gets turned. Just another monster for us to kill. The more the merrier as far as I'm concerned.'

I curse Rage, not for the first time, and stride towards him. 'Let the kid go,' I tell him, before he crushes the boy's skull.

'Why?' he laughs. 'Do you want to fight me?'

'No. But you know the rules—we need to check kids out before we destroy them.'

Rage scowls. 'I hate rules.'

'Tough. If you don't obey them, I'll tell Dr Oystein and we'll see how welcome you are at County Hall then.'

Rage mumbles something to himself, then lets the boy go. The kid immediately sets after Reilly, every bit as anxious to sink his fangs into a living human's brain as the adults are. I tackle him and easily stop his charge. I pull out the cuffs which I've brought along especially for this and slip a pair on to his wrists. Letting go, I push him to the ground, then snap another pair shut around his ankles. As the boy struggles furiously to break free, mewling miserably, I assess the situation.

Shane is back in the thick of things. He looks ashamed and so he should. A sheepish Jakob has resumed his position and is protecting Reilly again. Ashtat and Rage are picking off the last few adult reviveds. Carl has cuffed a girl even younger than the boy and is moving in on the last remaining child, another boy, this one not far off my age.

It's plain sailing now.

A minute later every zombie has been dispatched except for the three kids. As the rest of the Angels brush themselves down and give each other high-fives, I examine the cuffed prisoners, searching their thighs and arms for c-shaped scars. Dr Oystein spent decades injecting children with a vaccine which would help them fight the zombie gene if infected. If we find any child with the mark, we take them back to County Hall in case they revitalise further down the line.

Sadly, none of these three bears the scar of hope. They're regular reviveds, damned from the moment they were turned. I steel myself, offer up a quick prayer, then finish them off one by one. I feel sick every time I do this. I know they're undead killers, no different to any of the adult zombies that I've put out of their misery, but it still feels wrong.

I could ask one of the others to do it – Rage has no qualms about ripping the brain from a young zombie's head – but this is a hard world and Master Zhang has warned us that each one of us needs to toughen up if we're going to thrive and be of use to Dr Oystein. So I grit my teeth and force myself to push through with the dirty deed. I just hope, if God is watching, that He understands and forgives me, though I'm not sure I'll ever be able to forgive myself.

'Nice work,' Rage says when I'm done. He offers me his hand to high-five but I ignore him.

'I'm going to take that chain and help Reilly shove it up your arse,' I bark at Shane.

'I screwed up,' he winces. 'I'm sorry. It won't happen again. But my dad gave me that chain. It's all I have left of either of my parents.'

'Bullshit,' Rage snorts. 'I saw you take it from a shop last week.'

The pair burst out laughing. 'You shouldn't have told her,' Shane giggles as I glower at him. 'I had her going. She'd have melted and pardoned me.'

'*I* wouldn't have,' Reilly snarls, removing his helmet. 'My bloody *life* was on the line. I haven't been vaccinated. There's no coming back for me if I get turned. You risked my safety over a bloody chain that you can replace any time?'

Shane's smile fades. 'I really did screw up. I lost my head for a minute. I'm sorry, Reilly, honestly I am.'

'You'd better be,' Reilly says stiffly. 'And note this, you little thug—if anything like that happens again, I'll kill you. Even if I get bitten or scratched, I'll make it my job to stab you through the brain before I turn. Understand?'

Shane nods and averts his gaze.

'Apart from that, we did brilliantly,' Rage cheers, clapping loudly. 'Now let's go tell Master Zhang how we fared and ask Ciara to rustle us up some delicious brain stew. I don't know about you guys, but killing always makes me hungry.'

Rage licks his lips, the others laugh and cheer, then we trudge back to County Hall, experiment concluded, skills honed, one step closer to our hellish graduation.

THREE

We report back to Master Zhang, who's waiting for us in one of the rooms where he trains his recruits. He's angry when he hears what Shane and Jakob did. He's always stressing the need to focus and obey a direct order.

'No rest tonight,' he snaps at them. 'I want to see both of you here at lights out. I will work you through the night and it will not be a workout that you forget in a hurry.'

Shane pulls a face but Jakob only nods glumly.

'What about the others?' Zhang asks Reilly. 'Did they perform to your satisfaction?'

'Yeah. I don't have any complaints. They looked sharp.'

Our mentor sniffs, then waves us away. Shane hesitates. 'Master, I don't want to make a big deal of it, but I was injured. I think I might need a spell in a Groove Tube.'

'Let me see.' Zhang examines Shane's stomach and shoulder. The shoulder's no biggie, but the zombie dug quite deeply into the lining of his stomach. No guts are oozing out but it's bloody down there. 'Does it hurt?' Zhang asks.

'Yes,' Shane says.

'Good.' Zhang pokes one of the wounds and Shane cries out and doubles over. 'You will avoid the Groove Tubes. You will suffer your injuries and learn from the pain. Understand?'

'Yes . . . Master,' Shane wheezes.

'Now get out of here, all of you,' Zhang says. 'I am expecting another group for training soon, and hopefully they will pay more attention to my instructions than you.'

We bow and take our leave. Shane limps along,

gingerly massaging the flesh around his stomach. 'I bet the cuts get infected,' he mutters.

'It will serve you right if they do,' Ashtat says. 'You let us down and put Reilly's life in danger.'

'What about cancer boy?' Shane snaps. 'Jakob screwed up too.'

'Yes,' Ashtat says. 'But he screwed up trying to save a friend's life, not because he was worried about what would happen to an item of cheap jewellery.'

Shane glares at Ashtat and starts to retort.

'Leave it, big boy,' Rage chuckles, slapping Shane's back. 'They're right, you're wrong. Live with it, get over it, move on. Now, who's coming with me to get some stew?'

Everyone says they'll tag along with Rage, except me.

'I'm heading back to our room,' I tell them.

'Don't be a killjoy,' Carl frowns. 'Come with us. We did well in there apart from a couple of hiccups. Join the celebrations.'

'No, you're all right, I'm fine.'

'Suit yourself,' Carl says, irritated. They head off in search of Ciara, a close, united pack of friends. I

31

stare after them longingly, wishing I could belong, but at the same time knowing why I keep myself separate.

It's been a month since Dr Oystein fished me out of the Groove Tube after my fall from the London Eye and my run-in with the inhuman baby. When I'd dried off and he'd filed down my fangs and pumped my insides clean, I told him about my adventures, the monstrous baby and the dreams I'd had when I was alive of creatures just like it.

Dr Oystein is always hard to read, but my description of the baby didn't seem to come as a great shock. I think he already knew about the existence of such beings. My dreams, on the other hand, disturbed and intrigued him in equal measure. He made me recount them as clearly as I could.

'You are sure the babies in your nightmares were exactly the same as this one?' he asked. 'You are not imagining the similarity?'

'No,' I told him. 'I had the dreams all of my life, as far back as I can recall, until I was killed and stopped sleeping. I'm sure this baby was the same, not just because of the way it looked, but how it spoke and what it said.'

I told the doc how Owl Man had asked about my dreams when he came to visit me before the zombie uprising. That troubled him even more.

'I did not know that you had seen our owl-eyed associate before your encounter in Trafalgar Square,' he murmured.

I shrugged. 'I never thought to mention that. It didn't seem important. Do you know who he is?'

The doc nodded.

'What's his name?'

'That is irrelevant.' He smiled. 'I actually prefer Owl Man—it suits him better. That is how I will refer to him from now on.'

I wanted to learn more about Owl Man and the babies, but Dr Oystein said it was not yet time.

'Please be patient. I will share all the information that I possess with you, as I vowed when you first came here, but you must trust me to fill in the blanks as I see fit. I want to think about this first, what the nightmares might signify, how they link in with everything else.'

I told him I thought that the dreams had been sent to me by some higher force, so I'd see there were hidden, inexplicable depths to the world, and be more inclined to believe that the doc was telling me the truth when I came here.

'If that is the case,' Dr Oystein said softly, 'there is more to you than I first suspected. None of the other Angels had such dreams when they were alive. If God shared a premonition with you, there must be a reason for it. Perhaps you have a crucial role to play in the war with Mr Dowling.'

'Is that a good thing?' I asked.

He made a low, rumbling noise. 'I cannot say for sure. I know only that such responsibility is a frightening prospect. I have had to deal with it for decades. I do not wish to scare you, but I have to say that I would not wish such a burden on anyone.'

Then he kissed my forehead tenderly and sent me back to my room, telling me that he would consider what I'd told him and do all that he could to help me comprehend my path and steer me along it as best he could.

FOUR

I return to my room, change clothes, then scan the books on my shelves. I don't have a lot of stuff. Spare clothes, an iPod, some video games, a few nice watches and the books. I don't feel the need to cram my share of the room with personal items. London is an open city these days. Any time I want anything, I can simply go out and find it.

The others are the same. Nobody has bothered to clutter up their shelves or store goods in the many niches of County Hall. Carl has lots of fancy gear because he's into fashion, Shane has stacks of gold chains because he thinks they're cool, and Ashtat has hundreds of boxes of matches which she uses to make her brilliantly detailed models—she's currently working on one of Canary Wharf, her most ambitious project yet. Jakob has virtually nothing apart from some small photos of his family which he found in his mother's purse after she'd been killed along with his dad and sister.

My books are all about art and sculpture. If you'd told me when I was alive that I'd one day be an avid reader of such volumes, I'd have sneered. But time drags here. It's fine when we're training or on a mission, but otherwise we're stuck inside, staring at the walls.

The others play games and watch movies, but I've been keeping myself distant from my fellow Angels. Films don't hold the same appeal for me as they used to. Video games are the same. I haven't ditched them completely, but I can't spend a lot of time on them. I still listen to music, but my ears are so sensitive that I have to play the songs low, and where's the fun in that?

Art, on the other hand, has started to appeal to me. Mum was big into art and often tried to pass on her love of it to me. I resisted, in large part because I knew that Dad was scornful of it. He thought artists were pretentious wasters and I didn't want him looking down his nose at me.

My encounters with Timothy Jackson changed my view. His drawings of zombies fascinated me and I found myself thinking about them, the styles he had adopted, how they worked in different ways. I studied his paintings for a long time, then visited a few galleries to compare them with the work of other artists.

I started looking through the books in gallery shops. I wouldn't have dared go into such places in the old days. I'd have been afraid that the staff would laugh at me, or think I was just there to steal. But now there are only zombies to bear witness, and they couldn't care less about idle browsers.

I hadn't planned to read any of the books in detail, but the more I learnt, the more I could appreciate the pictures in them, as well as those hanging on the walls of the galleries. I lugged a couple of art books back to flick through, and soon my shelves started to fill up. There's no problem finding new volumes—here are loads of shops in London and they're open for business twenty-four hours a day, no credit card or cash required, and only the odd zombie bookseller or two to contend with.

Dr Oystein likes us to rest at night, to lie in our beds and act as if we're asleep. I read during that time, rather than just lie in the dark and count the seconds as they slowly tick by. No complaints from the others about my reading light—a few of them read as well, or play hand-held video games.

I used to be a slow reader but I've been speeding up recently. In the beginning I tended to choose books with lots of pictures in them, but now I've moved on to thick textbooks. I don't finish everything that I start, but when a book grabs my interest, I can plough through it pretty niftily.

So what am I in the mood for today? I study the titles, pick up a few, read the blurb on the back covers, then replace them. Until I come to *The*

Complete Letters of Vincent Van Gogh. I don't recall bringing this back, and it's a monster, so I'm sure I would have remembered. Frowning, I slide it free of the books around it and a note falls out. It's from Carl.

I saw you reading a book about Van Gogh. My dad had a copy of this in his library and often raved about it. I thought you might like to give it a go. Let me know if it's any good and I might try it myself.

I scowl at the note. I don't like it when people do nice things for me. I never know how to react. I suppose I'll have to thank Carl now—if I don't, I'll look like a mean-spirited cow. Why couldn't he have just told me about the book and let me find it for myself? Bloody do-gooder.

I think about dumping the book in the bin, but that would make me look childish and ungrateful. Besides, Van Gogh *is* one of my favourite artists and it sounds like a good read. Grumbling softly, I head to bed and settle down for a few hours of solitary reading.

I quickly get into the letters and time flies by. Carl

has picked a winner. On the one hand that annoys me, because it means I won't be able to jeer at him for giving me a piece of crap to read. But on the other hand I'm delighted to have discovered a brilliant new book, and I soon forget about Carl and having to say thank you and everything else.

A soft voice brings me back to the real world. 'I never thought I'd see B Smith lost in a book.'

I jump slightly – I had no idea that anyone had entered the room – and glance up. It's my old teacher, Mr Burke, standing in the doorway, beaming at me. 'I've always had a soft spot for nutters who cut their ears off,' I growl, carefully closing the book and setting it aside. 'Besides, this is a great read. I might have studied harder if I'd been pushed towards these sorts of books in school.'

'No,' Burke laughs. 'You wouldn't have given it a chance. You were a busy girl, so many slacker friends, so many things not to do with them. They wouldn't have been impressed if you'd started reading books instead of hanging out with them on street corners.'

Burke crosses the room, picks up the book and

flicks through it. He looks much older than he did in school, bags under his eyes, hair almost completely grey now. I never had a crush on Burke, but as teachers went, he was a bit of all right. Now he looks like a broken old man.

'I always meant to give this a try,' Burke says.

'You'd heard about it?'

'Yes. I was never much of an art buff. Biographies were my poison. *Seven Pillars of Wisdom*—now *that* was a book. But Van Gogh's letters were famous. I don't suppose I'll get time to read them now. I can't stay up all night like some undead people I can name.'

'I could always bite you,' I joke. 'Get Dr Oystein to vaccinate you first. You might turn into one of us. Then you can stay up as late as you like.'

'I've already been vaccinated,' Burke says, sitting on the bed next to mine, the one Jakob sleeps in.

'You have?' I sit upright and stare at him.

'I asked Dr Oystein to give me the shot not long after I started working for him.'

'Why?' I cry. 'You know what it means, don't you?

Unless you get infected, the vaccine will attack your system and melt you down. You'll be dead within the next ten or fifteen years.'

Burke shrugs. 'It's unlikely I'll last that long. There's a far greater probability that I'll be snagged by a zombie. If they don't eat my brain and I turn, I'd like the chance to revitalise. I know most adults don't, but still, better some hope than none at all.'

I shake my head. 'And what if you don't get bitten or scratched?'

Burke smiles. 'Then I'll miss out on old age. I wasn't looking forward to it anyway. I'd rather go in my prime, young, virile and full of life.'

'Too late,' I mutter. 'You missed that boat years ago.'

Burke laughs out loud then leans forward. 'How have you been, B? I haven't seen much of you since you returned.'

It's my turn to shrug. 'Fine. I've settled in. Learning lots. Training hard. Doing my bit for the cause.'

'Have you been on a mission yet?'

'Only scouting or training missions close to County Hall.'

The Angels do a lot of routine scouting, searching the streets and buildings of London for survivors—if we find any, we offer them a safe home at County Hall. We're also on the lookout for Mr Dowling and his mutants, as well as any human soldiers who might be on patrol. And, of course, we hunt for brains. We need regular supplies if we're to stay in control of our senses. Certain Angels do nothing except scour hospitals, schools and public buildings in search of corpses whose skulls they can scrape clean of brains to bring back for the pot, but all of us are expected to pitch in to some extent. One of the less exciting chores which everyone has to share.

I like getting out of County Hall when we go scouting, but it's an unpleasant sensation at the same time because we never know what we're going to run into, if Mr Dowling or his mutants will pop up, or if human hunters will set their sights on us. I crossed swords with some of them before I found my way here, the American Barnes and his buddies. There are others, bored survivors who pass the time by notching up kills. Not that they consider it killing. I mean, zombies are already dead, so it's no big deal to them.

The others in my group have been on more serious missions, where they've escorted humans out of London, or gone into dangerous areas with orders to carry out specific tasks. But Rage and I haven't been allowed on any of those yet.

'What about in your down time?' Burke asks.

I nod at the book. 'I've been making up for all those years when I never read anything other than porn stories online.'

Burke blinks. 'You're joking, aren't you?'

'Nothing wrong with a bit of sauce,' I smirk.

'Only if you're an appropriate age,' Burke huffs.

'Don't get all grown-up on me,' I snap. 'I had unlimited access to the internet from the age of ten or eleven. You think I wasn't curious? You think anyone my age didn't have a look to see what all the fuss was about? It wasn't like when you were a kid.

The world was our oyster. We could find out about anything.'

'I suppose,' he sighs, then smiles again. '*The world was our oyster.* You never used a phrase like that in the old days. All that reading must be rubbing off on you.'

'Of course it is. I'm not thick.'

'No,' Burke agrees. 'And never were. Even when you acted it.'

Burke picks up the book and looks at it closely again. He's obviously come to discuss something with me. I've an idea what it is but I don't say anything. I'm not going to make things easy for him. That's not my style.

'I don't want this to come out the wrong way,' Burke says hesitantly. 'And I'd hate to be classed as a teacher who ever discouraged reading. But are you maybe spending a bit too much time here on your own with your head stuck in a book?'

'No,' I answer shortly.

Burke chuckles, then sets the book aside and gets serious. 'What's wrong, B?'

'Nothing. I'm peachy.'

'No. You're not. Dr Oystein noticed and brought it to my attention.'

'Noticed what?'

'You returned to the fold after that incident with the baby,' Burke says, 'but you haven't made any effort to fit in with the other Angels. You don't socialise or hang out with your room-mates.'

'Maybe I don't like them,' I sniff.

'I doubt that's the case,' he says. 'If it was, you could simply ask to move in with a different group.'

'I thought that wasn't allowed. Dr Oystein tells us where to bed down.'

'When you first come here, yes. But if Ashtat and the others are still getting on your nerves after this much time, he'll be happy to let you switch. But they're not the problem, are they?'

'Rage is a pain,' I mutter.

'You don't get on with him?'

'I don't trust him. Never have, never will.'

'But the others?' Burke presses.

I shrug stiffly.

'If you tell me what's troubling you, I might be able to help,' he says kindly. 'A problem is never as bad as it seems if you share it with a friend.'

'But I don't need a friend,' I mumble. 'I don't *want* one. I don't mind working with the Angels, but I don't want to make friends with them.'

'Why not?' Burke asks, surprised.

'I'd rather be alone,' I say quietly.

Burke frowns, trying to make sense of me.

'It's not that complicated,' I snicker.

'It is to me,' Burke says. 'I'd have thought that someone in your position would give anything to find a friend.'

'What's so bad about my position?' I bark.

'Well, you're undead,' he says. 'Living people want nothing to do with you. Regular zombies have no interest in you either. There aren't many people left who could ever be tempted to give a damn about you. If you spurn the advances of the Angels, you're unlikely to find a friend anywhere else.'

'But I just told you I don't want any friends,' I remind him.

'You must,' Burke insists. 'You can't want to be all alone in the world.'

'I bloody well do,' I snort.

'Why?'

'Because it's simpler that way.' I reconsider my words and try again. 'Because it's safer.' I look down at my hands, at the bones sticking out of my fingers, remembering the blood that has stained them. 'You weren't there in the school when the zombies attacked. You were off sick that day. You didn't see us as we raced for freedom. You didn't see so many of my friends die, Suze and Copper and Linzer and . . .

'You weren't there when Mr Dowling invaded the underground complex either. You didn't see the zom heads tear into Mark or hear their death screams when Josh caught up with them. You didn't smell their burning flesh in the air.

'You weren't with me when all those people were killed in Trafalgar Square. Or when Sister Clare and her supporters marched into the belly of Liverpool Street Station. Or when Timothy was butchered.'

'I've seen terrible things too,' Burke says sadly.

'I'm sure you have. But I've *only* seen terrible things since I regained my mind. I've found death everywhere I've turned, or death has found me. I'm not saying I'm a jinx—I don't think I'm that important. But this is death's world now and I've run into the Grim Reaper every time I've turned a corner or paused for breath. Well, not actual breath, obviously, but you get the picture.'

I meet Burke's gaze at last. 'Pretty much everyone I've known and cared about has died or been taken from me. I'm sick of it. I don't want to endure the pain again. The Angels will be killed, I'm sure of it. Dr Oystein will get ambushed by Mr Dowling and his mutants. You'll be turned or slaughtered. It will all go tits up somewhere along the line.

'I don't want to feel anything when that happens. I don't want to lose friends or loved ones. I want to be able to get on with things and find somewhere else to hole up until death swings by again. I'd rather be a loner than feel lonely.'

Burke's eyes fill with pity. 'B . . .' he croaks.

'Don't,' I stop him. 'You came for answers and I've given them to you. Now leave me alone. It's all I ask of you. It's all I ask of anyone.'

Then I pick up the book, open it and stare at the words until Burke gets up and silently slips away, leaving me by myself. Not the way I like it really. Just the way it has to be if I'm not going to go crazy and lose myself to grief and madness in this harsh, unforgiving abattoir of a world.

FIVE

Getting ready to head out on another scouting mission. I was hoping Master Zhang would give us something meatier to deal with, but no, it's just another sweep of the area, this time around Covent Garden. There are lots of streets set back from the market, crammed with flats. We've been through there before, but repetition is nothing new.

We don't take any weapons when we head out, but we dress in heavy clothes and gloves to protect our skin from the sun. We also slap on loads of suntan lotion. Our clothes have been individually prepared for us, holes cut away to reveal our wounds and the wisps of green moss which signify to other zombies that we're undead like them.

I study the hole in my chest as I twist my jacket round. I've got so used to it that I can't really remember what it was like before. I hated being one tit short of a full set to begin with. Now I couldn't give a toss.

'I have said it before but I will say it again,' someone murmurs behind me. 'You are a most remarkable example of a zombie, Becky Smith.'

I turn, smiling, to face Dr Oystein. The doc never changes much. He favours a light grey suit, neatly ironed white shirt and a snazzy tie. His thin brown hair is shot through with grey streaks and carefully combed. His deep brown eyes are as calm and warm as always.

'I bet you say that to all the girls,' I chuckle.

'Only you,' he vows, then reaches out to adjust my coat around the hole where my heart used to be. 'There. Perfect.' He cocks his head to examine my face.

'Burke told you what I said, didn't he?' I pout.

'Of course. If it is any help, I understand. You are not the first to stand alone, to avoid the complications of company. I went through such a spell myself. It lasted several years. I figured, if I could train myself to feel nothing for anyone, I could never be hurt again, the way I was hurt when my family was so savagely taken from me.'

'How'd you get on with that?' I ask.

'Fine,' he says. 'I found it surprisingly easy to sever all emotional ties and distance myself from those I worked with.'

'Then why did you start caring again?' I frown.

'Instinct compels many reviveds to stay with those they knew in life,' Dr Oystein replies. 'But I do not think they truly care about those people. They have lost their souls, so they have no reason to give a damn. After a time, I realised I was behaving the same way as a revived. I came to think that God would not have restored my senses only for me to act as if I was still an unfeeling beast.

'Life was wonderful when we were alive,' the doc

continues. 'We could love, procreate, bond. The downside was that we could be hurt too. But we endured the pain because the joy was so intense.

'I won't pretend that nothing has changed. We cannot love the way we once did. Everything now is a resemblance. But even a vague, loving forgery is better than experiencing only the emptiness of the damned.'

'I'm not sure I agree with you,' I say solemnly. 'It'd be different if I didn't expect to lose some of you guys any time soon. But if I was to place a bet, I wouldn't give any of you more than six months, a year tops.'

'Even though I have survived more than a hundred years already?' he asks.

'Things were different then. The world made sense. It worked. Now it's just death, destruction and loss. We're all for the chop, and I don't want to care when you, Burke or anyone else gets ripped away from us.'

'What about our response if *you* are taken?' the doctor asks quietly. 'Will you care if nobody mourns your loss, if we wipe you from our thoughts and carry on as if nothing has happened?'

'Not in the least,' I say chirpily. 'When I go, I'm gone. Makes no difference to me whether you lot celebrate or wail for a week.'

Dr Oystein nods glumly. 'As you wish. Like I said, I do understand. If you do not seek friendship, we will not force it on you. No Angel needs to care for their colleagues in order to slot in with them.

'But I do care, B, and I will continue to. Billy Burke cares about you too, and quite a few more. If you ever change your mind and crave a friend, we will be here for you. Always.'

'Unless you're killed before me,' I note.

'Touché,' he smiles. Then, smile fading, he reaches out and touches my cheek, briefly but lovingly. 'Be careful out there, B. Come home safely to us.'

He turns and leaves. I want to call him back and accept his offer of friendship, drop my guard, have at least one person in the world that I can feel close to.

But I don't.

I can't.

I won't.

I remember my friends from school. My parents. Mark. Timothy. The pain I felt at their loss. And I make a vow to myself, not for the first time since I returned to County Hall.

Never again.

SIX

We patrol the streets, entering every building we come to, checking it thoroughly. Zombies are in many of them, sheltering from the sun. We gently edge past the resting reviveds and head up flights of stairs, exploring the upper levels, looking for attics or locked doors.

We haven't found any survivors while I've been with the Angels, but lots of humans were rescued before I joined, and a few have been unearthed by other search squads since. They've had to be cunning to survive so long in a city where death is almost a certainty.

Reviveds rely heavily on their sense of smell and hearing. To outwit them, the people with the smarts douse themselves in perfume or aftershave – those smells mean nothing to a zombie, they only react to natural human scents – and wear soft shoes or slippers. The really sly ones also wrap bandages round their stomach and chest to dull the sounds of their heartbeat and digestive system, shave off their hair so they don't sweat as much and take other inventive, anti-detection measures.

The gutsier survivalists realised that once a zombie has given a building a once-over, it usually doesn't check again, unless it was accustomed to double-checking spaces when it was alive, for instance if it was a security guard. So some of the humans have made their bases in buildings which zombies frequent, the reasoning being that they're the safest places in London, since the inhabitants won't scour their own lair. Also, other reviveds recognise and respect a fellow zombie's home, and they almost never trespass. We're not sure why, it's just the way they're wired.

Angels on earlier missions to find survivors never bothered to check a building that was home to a nest of reviveds. Now, having been clued in by those we've rescued, we're more thorough.

'Oh what fun,' Rage grumbles as we exit another block of flats with nothing to show for the time spent panning around inside.

'Patience is a virtue,' Ashtat says.

'What's so special about the living anyway?' Rage sniffs. 'Why should we care about them? If they find their way to County Hall, fair enough, it would be rude not to let them in. But we could be tracking down mutants, turning the tables on hunters, kicking Mr Dowling's arse. This is a waste of our time.'

'Yeah,' Shane says, backing up his buddy as he normally does.

'Don't act like an infant,' Carl snaps. 'We're fighting this war for the sake of those who are still alive.'

'Sure,' Rage says, 'but there are millions in camps or on islands dotted around the world. What does it matter if we rustle up a few more? It's not going to make a difference.'

'It will to those we rescue,' Ashtat says.

'Well, *duh*!' Rage snorts. 'I'm talking about the bigger picture. That's what we're supposed to be looking at, right? The doc told us that the minor battles being fought across the globe are meaningless. The fight here, between us and the clown's forces, is the only real game in town. So why aren't we focusing on that? We should be too busy to play at being Good Samaritans.'

Shane nods fiercely. 'What he said.'

Ashtat and Carl scowl at Rage and Shane, but don't come back with an argument because they can't think of one. I'm not bothered. It doesn't matter to me. I just do what I'm told and try not to think too much. That should be the end of the debate, a win for Rage, but then, breaking his usual moody silence, Jakob speaks up.

'I think it's to remind us that we were once human.'

We stare at the thin, pale boy. He doesn't speak very often. It's easy to think of him as a mute.

'I forget sometimes,' he says softly. 'I find it hard

to recall my life before this. It seems like I've been an undead creature for as long as I can remember.'

'So what?' Rage asks when Jakob falls silent again.

'When I feel distant from my humanity,' Jakob whispers, 'I think about linking up with Mr Dowling and his mutants. From all the reports, they have a grand time, going wherever they like, killing as they please, not caring about anyone except themselves. It must be liberating to be that brutal. The world has fallen. The walking dead have taken over. We don't neatly fit into one camp or the other. Why not throw in our lot with the clown and his crew, kill off the remaining humans and enjoy the party for the next few thousand years?'

'Blimey,' Rage laughs. 'And I thought *I* had a dark side.'

Jakob shrugs, wincing at the pain that brings to his battered, cancer-ridden body. 'That's just the way my mind wanders. Am I the only one who has thought such things?'

He looks around and everyone drops their gaze, except for Rage, who nods enthusiastically.

'Dr Oystein sees through us,' Jakob says. 'He knows all that we imagine. He can't rely on our unwavering support, because any one of us could give into desperation and temptation, and change sides.

'I think the searching, the rescues and escorting survivors to safe havens outside London are to keep us in contact with the memories of what it was like to be alive. Because if we lose those, or if they come to mean nothing to us, what's to hold us in place? Why should we bother to stay loyal?'

There's a long silence as we think about that. Jakob might not say much, but when he does speak, he tends to have something worth saying.

'Is that why you've been so distant recently?' Rage asks me. 'Are *you* thinking about stabbing us in the back and heading over Mr Dowling's way?'

'You're the only one I'd stab,' I smirk. 'I'd leave the others for the clown and his posse.'

'Then you *have* been thinking about it,' he challenges me, bristling.

'I think about all sorts of things,' I purr, baiting

him, unable to resist the opportunity to get under his skin.

'If you ever –' he starts to say, raising a finger to point at me warningly.

'Rage,' Ashtat interrupts.

'Don't stick up for her,' Rage barks. 'We won't have *girl power* here. If this little –'

'Shut up,' Ashtat says calmly, 'and look to your right.'

Rage glares at her but does as she commands. I see his eyes widen, so I look too.

There are a couple of people on the street, no more than ten metres ahead of us. They've come out of the remains of a shop. It's a woman and a young child. The woman is holding the child in her arms. I'm not sure if it's a boy or a girl.

But I'm sure of one thing, by the way their chests rise and fall, by the smell of the perfume they've coated themselves with, by the terror in the woman's eyes when she spots us.

They're alive.

SEVEN

For several seconds nothing happens. We stare at the woman and her child and she stares back. The child's face is turned into the woman's chest. I don't know if it's aware of us or not.

Ashtat lifts her hands over her head and calls out softly, 'We're not going to hurt you.'

The woman bolts the instant Ashtat moves. Not back into the shop, where we could trap her. Instead she turns and dashes along the street.

We start after her as a pack, acting instinctively. Carl stops us with a curt and commanding, 'Wait!'

As the rest of us pause, Carl jogs forward a couple of steps, then leaps. He lands not far behind the fleeing woman and immediately bounces into the air again, like a frog. He lands a few metres in front of her and she comes to a halt. Turns frantically, looking for an escape route. She spots an open door in a building and starts towards it.

'That's not a wise move,' Carl says calmly. 'There could be a dozen zombies on the other side of that door.'

The woman stops and stares at Carl. Then looks back at the rest of us. We're all standing still.

'What are you?' the woman gasps, taking another step away from Carl, edging closer to the door, caught in two minds.

'That's a long story,' Carl chuckles. 'All you need to know right now is that we mean you no harm. We're not going to attack you. We won't even detain you. If you're suspicious of us and don't want to talk, you can carry on down this street and we won't lift a finger to stop you. I'll just say two words to you before you go. *County Hall.*'

Carl shuffles out into the middle of the road. The woman licks her lips nervously, then starts to run. She thinks this is a trick. I don't blame her.

Nobody moves, even though we'll all hate it if we lose her. I say a silent prayer that she'll stop and look back. But then she turns a corner and disappears from sight. I feel my spirits sinking. I look around and everyone is staring glumly at the spot where she vanished, even Rage.

'Hard luck, Carl,' Ashtat says. 'At least you tried. I thought –'

'Wait a minute,' Carl hushes her. He's smiling hopefully. The fingers of his left hand are flexing slowly, as if trying to beckon the woman back. I don't think there's any chance of that, but I hold my peace along with the other Angels. I count inside my head, determined to give Carl the full minute he asked for. After that, I'll tell him to forget it, we can't win them all, maybe next time luck will be on our . . .

The woman edges back into view. First it's just her head, as she stares at us. Then she steps on to our street. She's still holding the child. It's looking at us now and I see that's it's a boy. Just four or five years old, but well drilled, silent as a butterfly.

The woman slips closer, studying the houses on either side, eyeing us uneasily. She stops a good distance away from Carl. She's trembling.

'You could have leapt through the air again and stopped me,' she says.

Carl nods.

'Why didn't you?'

'We don't want to trap you,' Carl says. 'If I tried to get in your way, you might run into me and scratch yourself. That would be bad.'

'Then you *are* a zombie?'

'A certain kind, yes.'

'Not the kind that eats brains?'

Carl laughs softly. 'Oh, we definitely eat brains, we have to. But we don't take them from the living. And we don't kill. We're your friendly neighbourhood kind of zombie.'

The woman doesn't smile but she stops shaking so much. 'And County Hall?' she asks. 'What did you mean?'

'It's where we're based,' Carl explains. 'If you don't want to come with us, that's cool, we won't force you. But if you're ever in need of allies or shelter, or looking for a way out of the city, come to County Hall and we'll help. You'll be safe there. It's the safest place in London.'

'Nowhere's truly safe,' the woman says.

'Not truly,' Carl concedes. 'But if you seek refuge there, and anyone wants to do you harm, they'll have to cut through us first.'

'What are you?' the woman asks again, frowning now.

'Like I said, that's a long story. But if you want to know *who* we are, I'm Carl Clay and these guys will be more than happy to introduce themselves if you let them.'

The woman wavers, takes a step back, thinks about it some more, then makes up her mind. 'I'm Emma,' she says. 'This is my son, Declan.'

'A pleasure to meet you, Emma,' Carl says, smiling broadly. 'Now, do you know any place around here where we could get a decent cup of coffee?'

And when he says that, despite herself, Emma returns the smile, and as sappy as it might sound, it's one of the most heart-warming things I've ever seen. Even for an undead, heart-deprived monster like me.

EIGHT

Carl wasn't joking about the coffee. He tells us that one of his uncles ran a small espresso bar in Kensington. Carl used to work there occasionally at the weekends, learning the trade. His parents thought it would be good for him, help keep his feet on the ground—he comes from a wealthy background and I guess they didn't want him losing touch with us common folk.

We find a deserted café, Carl takes Emma's order and heads in, delighted with himself. The rest of us wait on the street. Emma stands apart from us, still unsure she made the right choice when she came back. Declan is ogling us. He seems particularly fascinated by the hole in my chest.

'I'd let you poke about in there,' I smile at him, 'but it's dangerous.'

Declan blushes and hides his face. Emma laughs and rubs his head. 'No need to be afraid,' she coos. 'These people aren't going to hurt us. He was always shy,' she tells me. 'I used to encourage him to be more outgoing, but in this climate shyness isn't a bad thing. I haven't had any trouble keeping him quiet.'

I nod understandingly. 'Noise attracts the zombies.'

'Smells attract them too,' Ashtat mutters, looking around, worried. 'If any nearby reviveds get a whiff of that coffee . . .'

'Don't brick it,' Rage laughs. 'We can handle a few dumb reviveds if we have to.'

'But I'd rather not risk it,' Ashtat says and goes to see how Carl is getting on.

'Do other zombies attack you?' Emma asks me.

'Not usually,' I reply. 'But if we got in the way of a feed, they would.'

'Then we're putting you in danger.'

I shrug. 'We don't mind a little danger. It's what we're here for.'

Carl emerges with a mug of steaming hot coffee, beaming as if he'd delivered a newborn baby. Emma thanks him and reaches for it.

'Uh-uh,' he stops her and carefully lays the mug down on the ground for her to pick up. 'Best not to take any chances.'

'This is so weird,' she says, pulling a face as she retrieves the mug. 'If anyone had told me this morning that a zombie would be serving me coffee before the day was out . . .'

We all laugh, but quietly, so as not to draw attention. Then we head for Leicester Square, talking softly as we progress. We tell Emma about ourselves, how we differ from reviveds, the way we try to help living survivors, Dr Oystein and the set-up at County Hall. By the time we get to the small park at the heart of the West End and make ourselves comfy on a few of the benches, Emma is shaking her head with wonder.

'I never would have dreamt this was possible. I thought you were all killers.'

'Most of us are,' Ashtat says. 'Do not make the mistake of thinking you should give zombies a chance from now on. If you ever see one coming towards you, run. There are very few of our type around.'

'What about you guys?' Shane asks. 'How did you survive this long?'

'By being very careful,' Emma sighs. 'And with a lot of luck.'

'Are there more of you?' Carl asks. 'Do you want us to fetch the others and take them back to County Hall? Assuming you want to go there,' he adds quickly. 'No pressure. We'll understand if you'd rather stick to what you know.'

'Are you kidding?' Emma says bitterly. 'I hate what we've had to endure, the places we've had to stay, the loneliness. Of course we're coming with you. If I'd only known about you before . . .'

She starts to cry. The rest of us say nothing and look away awkwardly, waiting for the tears to pass. Declan makes a small whining sound and, when I glance at him, I see him stroking his mother's hair and kissing her cheek. I recall the monstrous babies from my dreams, and the all-too-real baby at Timothy's, and suppress a shudder.

'Sorry,' Emma moans when the tears finally pass. 'I've been holding those in for so long. I didn't want to cry before this. I was afraid I might not be able to stop once I'd started, that I might start howling with grief and rage.'

'Howling's not good in this city,' Shane notes. 'It draws a crowd.'

'Yes.' Emma wipes tears away and grins at us, embarrassed. 'Sorry,' she says again.

'No need to apologise,' Ashtat smiles. 'We would love to cry if we could.'

Emma blinks. 'You mean you can't?'

'Unfortunately not. We are, in most respects, dead. There are many things the undead can no longer do—cry, sweat, breathe.'

Emma shakes her head, amazed, and drains the last of her coffee. 'That was so good,' she says.

'I can make you some more if you'd like,' Carl offers.

'Not right now,' she says. 'Maybe in a while. I don't like to drink too much. I'm always afraid the smell might tip off the zombies. Does it?'

'I'm not sure,' Carl says. 'Most reviveds aren't good at association. That's why they don't link the smell of perfume or aftershave to the living. But I've seen some react to the scent of food before. I think they remember that only a living human would bother with food, since the walking dead don't eat. Well, except for brains obviously.'

'But you're safe with us,' Shane brags. 'You can have a barbecue if you like, here in the Square. We'll run off any nosy buggers who come sniffing round.'

Emma giggles. 'A barbecue! This is like a dream. I wish ...' She pauses and her expression darkens. 'I wish Shaun could have been here. He practically lived for barbecues. He was Australian. He grew up cooking outdoors.'

'Was Shaun your husband?' Ashtat asks delicately.

'No,' Emma grunts. '*He* left the picture long before the zombies struck, and good riddance to him. I hope he was one of the first to die and that it was painful and slow.' She glowers, then chuckles. 'I don't mean that really. But I certainly wouldn't shed any tears if I found out he was dead.

'Shaun was a friend of mine. We were together the day the zombies took over. He was a survival expert, he loved challenging himself in harsh terrains, he'd spend his holidays cheating death in hellholes around the world. I thought he was crazy, but he used to say a beach holiday was his idea of purgatory. He wasn't happy when he went away unless he staggered back bloody, bruised and exhausted.

'I was glad of his skills after the attacks,' she goes on. 'We wouldn't have lasted long without him. He taught us how to hide and forage. He studied the zombies, learnt about them, helped us stay one step ahead. I wanted to flee the city, but Shaun said we stood a better chance here, at least to begin with. I kept urging him to take us to one of the settlements in the countryside, or to try for an island, but he was sceptical. He didn't believe all of the reports on the radio. He wanted to let things settle. I also think he was reluctant to put his life in the hands of anyone else. He liked his independence.'

'Did the zombies get him?' I ask.

Emma nods. 'We picked up other survivors along the way. We numbered eight at our maximum. Shaun always told me not to let myself get too attached to them. He said if we ever got backed into a corner, we had to abandon the others and look after ourselves. He said we couldn't afford the luxury of friends any more.'

'Sounds like he knew what he was doing,' I mutter, thinking about my talk with Mr Burke.

'Yes,' Emma sighs. 'But he couldn't follow his own advice in the end. We lost a couple of members to attacks over the months. Another couple struck out for the countryside by themselves. A few more joined up. Shaun was always in command. He was a natural leader. Nobody in the group ever challenged him.

'One of the new guys was diabetic. He needed insulin. We were in a chemist's. Zombies were nesting on the upper floor. They chased us. The guy with diabetes got trapped. Shaun went back for him. He shouldn't have. If I'd done it, he would have bawled me out. But you could never tell Shaun anything.'

Emma starts weeping again but softly this time. 'That was a couple of months ago. Those of us who were left stayed together for a few weeks. Then the others decided to leave London. I hung on, remembering what Shaun had said. We've been alone since then, haven't we, Declan?'

The little boy nods stiffly. He's crying too now, but quietly, shivering in his mother's arms.

'You've done well to survive,' Jakob says softly. 'Shaun would be proud.'

Emma nods and sniffs. Carl chews on his lower lip, wanting to say something more to comfort the pair. Then he has a brainwave.

'Does Declan have any toys?' he asks.

Both Emma and Declan stop crying and stare at Carl. 'No,' Emma says. 'I pick up some things for him every now and then, if we're staying in one spot for a few nights, but we move around a lot and we can't carry much with us when we travel. Toys are pretty low on our list of priorities.'

'I figured as much,' Carl says, getting to his feet. 'We're not that far from Hamleys. Why don't I pop over there and find some really cool toys for him to play with in County Hall?'

'I'm not sure,' Emma says. 'I've passed by Hamleys a few times. It's full of zombies. I never dared go in.'

'They won't bother *me*,' Carl laughs and sets off, excited at the thought of exploring the different levels of the famous old toyshop.

'Do you want us to come with you?' Ashtat asks.

'No,' he says. 'Stay here and enjoy the sun. Emma and Declan will be safer in the open, with plenty of escape routes.'

'Hold on,' I stop him. 'I'm coming.'

'I don't need back-up,' he snorts.

'I'm sure you don't. Still, it can't hurt having someone to look out for you. And I can give you a hand bringing stuff back.'

Carl thinks about that and shrugs. 'OK, if you want. Just as long as we're clear that I'm the one who gets to choose.'

'Don't worry about it,' I say drily. 'I know better than to come between a boy and his toys.'

Carl starts to retort, then remembers that there's a young child present. He catches himself, grins sheepishly at Emma, then off we head in search of some toys that will hopefully bring a smile to the solemn boy's face.

NINE

'You didn't need to tag along,' Carl says as we exit the Square and head towards Regent Street.

'You shouldn't go off solo,' I grunt. 'Anything could happen to you.'

'Would you be bothered?' Carl asks.

I shrug. 'I don't want to have to explain your loss to Master Zhang.'

Carl smiles. '*You* went off by yourself after you fell from the London Eye.'

I haven't told them that Rage pushed me. They think I fell. I didn't even tell Dr Oystein. I'm not a tattletale. What happened on the Eye was between Rage and me.

'I'm a special case,' I mutter.

Carl looks at me sideways and smirks. 'I think you fancy me.'

'In your dreams.'

'That's why you've come. You can't bear to be parted from me.'

I fake a yawn. 'Yeah, that's it.' Then I tell him, 'Actually it's because of the book.'

He frowns. 'What are you talking about?'

'The book with the Van Gogh letters. It's great. You gave it to me, so I wanted to repay you.'

'It's no big deal,' he says. 'You could have given me a book in return.'

'I couldn't be arsed looking for one.'

He grins. 'Or you could have just said thanks.'

'Nothing says thank you better than saving a person's life,' I drawl.

Carl shakes his head. 'You're a strange one, Smith.'

'Am I?'

'Yes. I can't figure you out. I try being nice to you, and you clearly appreciate that or you wouldn't feel compelled to repay me. But instead of just accepting me as a friend, you have to turn it into something weird.'

'Nothing weird about it,' I grunt. 'I liked the book. This is my way of doing something nice for you in return.'

'You could simply be my friend,' Carl says.

'I'd rather save your neck.'

'Even though you don't like me?' he presses.

'I never said I didn't like you.'

'Then you do like me?'

'I never said that either.'

Carl stops and squints. 'Are you playing mind games with me?'

'No.' I roll my eyes. 'You're just a guy I work with, same as the others. I'm happy to keep things pleasant, but I don't want to do more than that. Friends aren't my thing.'

'Must be lonely up there in that tower,' Carl says.

'Suits me fine,' I retort. 'Now, are we sorting out those toys or what?'

Carl looks at me a beat longer, then shrugs and starts off again. He doesn't say anything else. I don't either. I didn't want to piss him off, but he kept asking until there was nothing else for it but to hit him with the truth.

After a short, uneventful journey, we stop outside Hamleys. Any time I passed by before, it was swarming with kids and tourists. Now it's no different to any other large building in this city, silent, no signs of life, just the occasional flickering shadow as zombies shift around inside.

'It's sad,' Carl says. 'It feels more like a graveyard than a toyshop now.'

'Do you want to try somewhere else?' I ask.

'No. The other places will be the same. I'll go look inside, see what I can rustle up. I might be a while— I always seem to turn into a big kid in here. Do you want to come with me, or do you want to browse by yourself?'

'Actually I think I'll stay out here and keep watch,'

I say, not wanting to go in and be confronted with all those toys, along with the realisation that no children will ever come to play with them again. 'I'll give you a shout if I spot anything.'

'Like what?' he laughs. 'Elephants?'

'Just get on with your job, *toy boy*,' I growl and move away from the door, out of his line of sight.

As Carl goes on the hunt for the perfect present, I shuffle along, away from the windows which are still packed with displays of toys that haven't been disturbed, until I come to a stretch of wall that I can lean against. I glance around idly, then study my fingerbones, picking at them, cleaning them. I keep them in good shape, but with all the training and fighting, they get scraped and chipped. The scuffs don't really bother me, but I like to keep them neat and tidy. I guess filing down the bones is the closest I get to polishing my nails these days.

As I'm digging at a thin crack in one of the bones, trying to scrape out the dirt, I hear something rustling to my left. I look up but can't see anything. Probably just a rat. I return my attention to my bones, but then there's a shuffling sound off to my right. I frown and step away from the wall, squinting. The sun's in my eyes. I raise a hand to shade them.

Something strikes the back of my neck and a surge of electricity crackles through me. Every muscle in my body goes haywire. I collapse instantly. I try to cry out with pain, but my mouth won't work. It's like I'm filling with sparks. Lights dance across my eyes and I go temporarily blind.

As my vision starts to clear, a man rushes towards me. A gag is shoved into my mouth. My hands are jerked behind my back and tied together. Someone else binds my legs. I want to scream for help, but I'm still spasming and the gag would stop me making any noises anyway.

The guy who bound my hands starts to jam a thick sack down over my head. He pauses before he covers my eyes and waits for me to focus on him. As I do, the world swimming slowly back into place around me, I spot his dark, grey-streaked hair and brown eyes, and I think it's Dr Oystein, that this is a test.

Then the man's features solidify and I realise it's not the doc. I don't know why I ever thought it was. The pair look nothing alike. This guy is much broader, with a menacing expression, and Dr Oystein never went around with a bullet stuck behind his right ear.

When I spot the bullet, everything clicks and I realise what's going on. I try to scream again, to at least alert Carl, even if it's too late for me. But the hunter knows his job. He's not in the habit of making mistakes.

'Hello again, my bizarre little beauty,' he whispers.

And, as he tugs the sack down over my face, thrusting me into darkness, I try screaming one last time, unsuccessfully willing myself to bellow his name out loud for all the world to hear.

'*Barnes!*'

TEN

My captors pick me up and hurry along the street with me. I try kicking out at them, but I'm expertly bound and my muscles are still throbbing from the shock. I've never been tasered before. I didn't think it would hurt so much. My head is ringing and it feels like I've been sucking batteries for a week.

I'm bundled into the back of a van and the doors slam shut. The engine starts and we lurch forward. It's been so long since I was in a moving vehicle, the sensation is strange. I get a bit nauseous. I never suffered from travel sickness when I was alive.

Maybe it has something to do with my altered hearing.

I've no idea what's going on. Barnes is a hunter. When I met him before, he was leading a small team, killing zombies for sport. I could understand that. But why kidnap me now instead of shoot me dead when he had the chance? Does he plan to torture me?

I wouldn't have thought he was the type. That day in the East End, when he realised I could think and speak, he let me go. He even threatened to eliminate one of his crew, Coley, a nasty piece of work who wanted to kill me despite the fact I wasn't like the other zombies.

But maybe I caught Barnes on a soft day. He might have thought about it since then and decided I was fair game. Perhaps he got tired of executing mindless zombies and wanted to experiment on one who could react to his taunts.

As I'm considering the nature of the man who now controls my fate, the sack is pulled free of my head. Barnes is squatting in front of me, grinning bleakly.

'I know you haven't forgotten me,' he says quietly in his American accent. 'You're in trouble and I won't pretend you're not. But I'm not figuring on killing you. If you play ball, you might get out of this alive. Now, do you want me to take out that gag?'

I nod sharply.

'If you try to bite me, I'll execute you,' he says, showing me a hunting knife. 'I'll dig this straight into your brain at the first snap of your teeth.'

I glare at Barnes as he reaches out and removes the gag, but slide my head backwards as soon as my mouth is free, away from his gloved fingers, to signal to him that I'm not going to strike. Barnes didn't bother with gloves the first time I met him, but I guess he's racked up the stakes a level and is getting much closer to zombies now. If you're gonna get hands-on with one of us, you need to be more cautious.

'How did you find me?' I snarl.

'I've been staking out Leicester Square and the area around it for several weeks,' he says. 'I guessed you – or those like you – would swing through sooner or

93

later. The Square might have fallen from grace, but it's still the heart of the city.

'I've seen you before,' he continues. 'A few times. But you were always part of a group. I didn't want to target you when you were with company. Too complicated. Always easier to pick off a stray.

'Actually I wasn't after you specifically,' he adds. 'Any one of you would have done. But I had a feeling it would be you. The universe works strangely that way. I don't believe in destiny, but coincidence is a far more complex beast than most people give it credit for.'

'God bless coincidence,' the driver laughs. 'I'm glad you didn't let me kill her all those months ago.'

'Coley?' I growl. Barnes's hunting partner wanted to shoot me when our paths first crossed. Barnes wouldn't let him. Rather, he said he'd let Coley shoot me, but that he'd disable him in return and leave him for the zombies as punishment.

'Guess you didn't think you'd be seeing me again,' Coley snickers.

'Not this side of Hell,' I snarl. 'I hoped a zombie would have ripped you apart by now.'

'Not this fleet-footed fox,' Coley boasts.

'I'm surprised you're still together,' I mutter. 'I thought you'd have gone your separate ways after what happened, Barnes threatening to shoot off your kneecaps and all.'

'Nothing more than a minor quarrel,' Coley says, glancing over his shoulder to show me his grin. He's sporting fancy designer glasses, the same as before. His straw-coloured hair is a bit longer. Both men are wearing army fatigues.

'A lovers' tiff?' I murmur, smiling back at Coley as best I can from my awkward position.

Coley's face darkens. 'I say we cut out her tongue.'

Barnes chuckles. 'Not yet. Our lords and ladies might want her to sing for them first.'

'What's going on?' I ask.

'You'll find out soon,' Barnes tells me.

'You won't like it when you do,' Coley cackles and takes a bend sharply, tyres squealing. Barnes almost topples on to me.

'Careful!' he barks.

'Don't worry,' Coley says. 'I'm in total control of this baby.' We hit a bump and Barnes is jolted into the air. Again he has to steady himself before he falls within range of my infectious teeth.

'I won't warn you again,' Barnes says.

'You're no fun,' Coley pouts but slows to a more reasonable speed.

Barnes scowls at the back of his partner's head, then leans in close to me. 'If it's any consolation,' he whispers so that only I can hear, 'I hate having to do this. It won't mean much to you, I know, but for what it's worth, I'm sorry.'

And the sad look he flashes me is far more worrying than any threat he might have made.

ELEVEN

We drive for what feels like twenty or thirty minutes. It involves a lot of zigzagging around crashed or abandoned vehicles, which slows us down. A few zombies hurl themselves at the vehicle every now and then, but they bounce off and are easily left behind. Coley swerves on other occasions to deliberately mow down zombies that are in his path. He whoops every time he hits one, sometimes pausing to reverse over them, trying to squash their heads.

Barnes sighs and purses his lips with disapproval, but says nothing, letting Coley have his grisly fun.

The van finally draws to a halt and Coley kills the engine. Having checked the mirrors to make sure the area is clear of the living dead, he hops out, trots round to the back and opens the doors. 'Here, kitty, kitty,' he purrs and reaches in for me. He grabs my feet and starts to pull me out.

'Wait until I gag her,' Barnes says.

'Don't,' I ask him as he leans towards me. 'I won't bite, I swear.'

'I believe you but I can't take any chances,' he says. 'It won't be for long, just until we can set you down.'

Barnes puts the gag back in place and secures it. Then he nods at Coley, who happily hauls me out of the van. I land on the ground with a thump. Coley kicks me while I'm down, hard in the ribs.

'Not such a tough girl now, are you?' he spits.

'There's no need for that,' Barnes says wearily, climbing out of the van and shutting the doors.

'Don't tell me you're going to shoot me just for kicking her,' Coley giggles.

Barnes frowns. 'Some days I wonder why I keep you around.'

'Because I'm good at what I do,' Coley says smugly, kicking me again. 'It's the same reason I put up with your righteous crap. We work well together. We need each other, much as it might pain either of us to admit it.'

Barnes cracks his knuckles and casts an eye over me. 'You take the legs,' he says. 'I'll take the upper body.'

'You sure?' Coley asks.

'Yeah. You'd keep dropping her on her head otherwise.'

Coley laughs with delight then picks up my legs. Barnes slips his hands under my shoulders and lifts. They juggle me around until they're comfortable, then start ahead. They're both strong men and they might as well be carrying a small dog for all the effort it takes them. Even so, I'm guessing they won't want to carry me too far – they're vulnerable with me in their hands, easy prey if zombies attack – and I'm proved right a minute later when they pass by the cool glass building of City Hall, head down to the bank of the Thames and take a left.

HMS *Belfast* is docked ahead of us. I came this way when I first trekked across from the east. There were people on the deck of the famous old cruiser, armed to the teeth. They shot at me before I could ask any questions, scared me off, made it clear they didn't welcome strangers. They're still up there and look to be just as heavily armed. But they don't fire at Barnes and Coley. It seems like they're expecting us.

The hunters carry me up the gangway. They don't say anything. Once onboard, they lay me down and take a step back. The people with the rifles press closer. There are at least a dozen of them, more spread across the deck. They look like soldiers although they're dressed in suits. They don't smile, just stare at me with distaste.

'Is this one of the speaking zombies?' a man in a suit and wearing shades like Coley's asks.

'Yeah,' Barnes replies.

'You finally came good and caught one,' the man sniffs.

'I swore that I would.'

'Took you long enough.'

Barnes smiles tightly. 'If you thought you could do better, you should have said so. I'd have been happy to spend my days lounging around here and let you go scour the streets instead.'

The man in the suit scowls. 'Think you're hot stuff, don't you, Barnes?'

Barnes shrugs. 'I'm just a guy who gets the job done. Now, are the lords and ladies of the Board ready to accept their delivery?'

'Wait here,' the man says. 'I'll go check.'

There's a short delay. Barnes and Coley stand at ease. The people with the rifles keep them trained on me, ready to blast me to hell if I show the slightest sign that I'm about to try to break free.

Eventually someone comes running towards us. 'Let me see! Let me see!' a panting man cries and the guards around us part.

I spot a fat man in a sailor suit prancing across the deck. The suit is too small for him and his stomach is exposed. It's hairy and there are crumbs stuck in the hairs.

The fat man crouches next to me and stares, eyes wide, lips quivering. He notes the hole in my chest and studies my face. His smile fades. 'It's a girl. I thought it would be a boy.'

'I didn't know you had a preference,' Barnes says. 'Does it make any difference?'

The fat man purses his lips. 'I suppose not. I just assumed . . .' He shrugs and smiles again. 'Make her talk, Barnes. Make her talk for Dan-Dan. I want to hear her before the others. I want to be the first.'

Barnes looks at the guard in the suit and glasses, who has followed behind the guy dressed like a sailor. The guard shrugs. Barnes carefully removes my gag and shifts out of my way.

The fat man nods at me, grinning like a lunatic. 'Come on, little girl. Talk for Dan-Dan. Let me hear you.'

I look *Dan-Dan* up and down, slow as you like, then smile lazily. 'You're about three sizes too large for that ridiculous suit, fat boy.'

Dan-Dan's jaw drops. Some of the guards smirk. Coley snorts with laughter. Barnes just stares at me.

'You ... you ...' Dan-Dan sputters. He starts to swing a hand at me, to slap me. Then he remembers what I am and stops. His smile swims back into place and he blows me a kiss. 'You're wonderful,' he gurgles. 'A spirited, snarling, she-snake. Everything I was hoping for and more. We're going to have so much fun with you, little girl.'

Dan-Dan lurches to his feet and claps his hands at Barnes and Coley. 'Don't stand there like fools,' he barks, going from buffoon to commander in the space of a few seconds. 'Bring her through to the Wardroom. The others are waiting and we're not renowned for our patience.'

As Barnes and Coley pick me up again – pausing only to stick my gag back in place – Dan-Dan sets off ahead of us. He waddles like a duck but there's nothing funny about him now. I'm in serious trouble here. And while the farcically dressed fat man is nowhere near as scary as Mr Dowling or Owl Man, he's probably more of a threat than either of them. Both of those freaks chose to let me run free, but I've a horrible feeling that Dan-Dan wants me for keeps.

TWELVE

Barnes and Coley carry me across the deck, down a flight of stairs, then towards the rear of the cruiser, which they refer to as the aft. Dan-Dan trots ahead of us, skipping at times, singing to himself.

Dan-Dan opens a door and we enter a long room dominated by a massive table. It could easily seat a couple of dozen people, but only five individuals are sitting around it. They're spread out, as if they don't want to sit too close to one another. There are ten guards in the room, standing by the walls, surrounding the table. All have handguns and are pointing them at me.

Coley chuckles uneasily. 'You guys want to lower those? If you fire off a shot accidentally, you might hit Barnes or me.'

'There will be no accidents here,' a woman at the table says. She's in her forties or fifties. Dressed to the nines, dripping in necklaces and diamonds. If she looked any posher, she'd be a queen.

Dan-Dan takes a seat and chortles. 'Lady Jemima is correct, as always. If we shoot you, it will be on purpose.'

Barnes ignores the veiled threat and helps Coley set me on my feet. 'Her name's Becky Smith,' he tells the six people at the table. 'She's one of the talking zombies.'

'It's true,' Dan-Dan gushes. 'I heard her speak on deck. She insulted me. I didn't like that—she's a naughty little minx who must be taught the error of her ways. But she can definitely speak.'

'We never doubted you, Barnes,' another man says. He's smartly dressed in a purple suit. He looks young, but there are faint wrinkles around his eyes when he smiles, which make me think he's older than he appears. 'We were just concerned that it was taking you so long to find one for us.'

Barnes shuffles his feet and pulls a face. 'I'm slow but sure.' It's an act. There's nothing slow about Barnes. But he's clearly wary of these people and their armed guards.

'Remove the gag,' one of the other men says. This one has an eastern European accent. He's dressed like a prince, crown and all.

'Yes, sir,' Barnes murmurs and reaches up to free my mouth. 'Be careful what you say to them,' he whispers. 'They don't have a sense of humour.'

I stare silently at my regally attired captors when the gag has been removed.

'Well?' Lady Jemima asks, twisting a diamond ring as she bores into me with her gaze.

'What?' I sniff and she stops turning the ring.

'Incredible,' she sighs.

'She spoke to me first,' Dan-Dan crows. 'Did you hear that, Luca?' he calls to the guy in the purple suit. 'I was first.'

'Mother would be so proud of you,' Luca purrs

sarcastically. 'If you hadn't thrown her to a zombie to save yourself, that is.'

Dan-Dan's face drops. 'I thought we weren't going to mention that again.'

Luca sniffs and leans towards me. 'Tell us about yourself, girl. Where are you from? How can you speak? Are there many more like you?'

I cock my head at him and don't answer. He studies me silently, then grins viciously. 'The next time you refuse to answer a question, I'll have one of my men cut off the little finger on your left hand. After that, it will be your head. I only believe in a single warning. So, unless you're keen to die today, talk.'

'There's not much I can tell you,' I say sullenly. 'I don't know how I can talk or why I'm different.' That's a lie, but I'm not going to rat out Dr Oystein to this pack of creeps. I think about saying I'm a one-off, but Barnes has seen me with other Angels. I have to be careful, lie cautiously, mix in a bit of truth.

'There are several of us that I know about. We wander around London together. We've been looking

for answers but haven't found any, so we've been getting by as best we can.'

'Does the girl need to eat brains?' the other woman
at the table asks. She's conservatively dressed in a dark
jacket and trousers. Grey hair. A pinched face. 'Ask
her if she needs to eat brains, Luca.'

'Ask her yourself,' Luca snaps.

The woman frowns. 'I don't want to talk to one of
them. She's a thing, not a person.'

'But you're happy for me to talk to her?' Luca
growls.

'You're more natural in situations like this,' the
woman simpers.

Luca barks a laugh. 'You're useless, Vicky. I don't
know how you got into Parliament so many times.'

'By being ruthless with people who displease me,'
Vicky says flatly.

'Peace,' the final man to speak says. He's the
oldest, a white-haired, thick-limbed guy. The others
quit squabbling immediately. The man rises and
crosses the room to study me up close. If I leant forward quickly, I could bite him. But it would be my

final act and he knows it. I don't smell any fear on him.

'My name is Justin Bazini,' he says. 'If you had the right connections, you would know what that name means. I'm a man of immense wealth and power. Those are Lords Luca and Daniel Wood, not as well off as my good self, but not short of a few shillings either.'

'What are shillings?' Dan-Dan asks jokingly.

Justin points at the overdressed woman. 'Lady Jemima. You probably saw her picture a lot in the fashion magazines when you were alive.'

'I didn't waste my time reading fashion mags,' I sniff.

He looks down at my clothes and smiles mockingly. 'Evidently not. Our other good lady is Victoria Wedge. I imagine you weren't the most political of creatures, so I don't suppose you –'

'I know who Vicky Wedge is,' I interrupt. 'I don't recognise the face but I know the name. My dad used to talk about her. He thought the sun shone out of her backside. Not too fond of foreigners, was she?'

'There is nothing wrong with foreigners,' Vicky Wedge says with an icy smile. 'As long as they are invited foreigners who can be of benefit to their adopted homeland. Was your father one of my supporters?'

'Yeah. He had the real hots for you. He always had a soft spot for bigots.'

I expect her to flush at the insult but she only laughs. 'What a charmless little beast. The perfect example of why I campaigned for chemical castration of the more vulgar, useless proletariat.'

'You surely did not campaign openly about such a controversial issue, did you?' the guy with the crown asks.

'No,' Vicky scowls. 'My spin doctors advised against it. They thought it might inspire some of the vile creatures to crawl to the polling stations to vote against me.'

'And, finally, the gentleman with the crown is The Prince.' Justin wraps up the introductions.

'No actual name?' I ask.

'I prefer not to use it,' The Prince says grandly. 'In

this world I am one of the last of my kind. One day I will be *the* last. People might as well get used to calling me by my title.'

'Not interested in being king?' I sneer.

'Oh no,' The Prince says. 'Nobody likes a king. But everyone loves a prince. I want to be loved. I *will* be loved.'

Justin returns to his seat and rocks back and forth as he addresses me. 'We are the Board. We happened to be together here in London when the world fell. Rather than flee, as so many in our position did, we stood firm and made this vessel our own, choosing it both because it's easier to defend than a landlocked building and because it's such a potent reminder of our glorious past.'

'Plus I've always liked big boats,' Dan-Dan giggles. 'Sailors are my favourite military personnel. Their uniforms are to die for.'

'We're going to run this world again one day,' Luca says.

'And run it the right way this time,' Vicky Wedge adds pointedly.

'From here?' I ask sceptically.

'Of course not,' Justin snaps. 'This is merely a temporary base. But we will maintain our position in London, you can be sure of that. Once the situation has stabilised and we've rid the streets of their zombie scum, we'll recover Downing Street and Buckingham Palace, and run the world from the heart of the great British Empire, as it always should have been.'

'*Rule Britannia*,' Dan-Dan sings at the top of his voice.

'I think the army might have something to say about that,' I mutter.

'Nonsense,' The Prince chuckles. 'Soldiers exist to be given orders. No military junta ever ruled for long. They will need leaders to guide them.'

'And you think you guys fit the bill?'

'Who else?' Justin challenges me. 'The other survivors of our stature, who might have provided competition, fled like frightened animals when the chips were down. Class will always triumph. We stood firm and that will be acknowledged.'

'You're cuckoo,' I sniff, ignoring Barnes's warning

to be careful about what I say. 'Money doesn't matter any more. You won't be able to buy your way into power again.'

'Foolish child,' Lady Jemima laughs.

'Ignorant brat,' Vicky Wedge adds snidely.

'Money will always be a factor,' Dan-Dan says, dropping the man-child act. 'Cash might not be worth what it was, but diamonds and gold hold their value no matter what.'

'We have plenty of those stored away,' Luca boasts.

'And we know where we can get more,' The Prince beams, rubbing his hands together greedily.

'In short,' Justin concludes, 'we're perfectly positioned to take control of the world. It will happen, there is no question of that. It's just a matter of when. And until then we're keen to kill time.' He's been drumming his fingers on the table. Now he stops and points at me. 'That's where *you* come in. Tell me, Miss Smith, do you have a taste for combat? If you don't,' he adds quickly before I can answer, 'fret not, dear girl, because you will develop one soon, once the killing begins . . .'

THIRTEEN

The members of the Board file out of the Wardroom, Dan-Dan moving swiftly to make sure he's at the head of the procession. Half the guards go with them. The other half keep their weapons trained on me.

'What's going on here?' I ask Barnes.

He doesn't answer. Instead it's Coley who says, 'Entertainment will always be a thriving industry. Our lords and ladies wish to be amused, and they have the funds in place to ensure those wishes are met.'

'You can't care about money now,' I mutter, again addressing my comments to Barnes. 'Those power-hungry leeches are doolally. We can never go back to the old ways.'

'I'm not too sure about that,' Barnes says softly. 'But no, I'm not in it for the money.'

'Then what?' I growl. 'The kicks? Do you like seeing zombies suffer?'

Barnes only stares at me.

'He has his reasons,' Coley says defensively.

'And they're mine to share or not,' Barnes barks.

'Easy, big guy,' Coley chuckles. 'I wasn't going to say any more.'

'What about you?' I sniff.

'I like the work and I like the perks,' Coley grins. 'There are women here who look kindly on brave soldiers like me. We have access to alcohol, drugs, anything we want. Power and wealth mean nothing to me. It's all about the fringe benefits.'

A guard comes to fetch us and leads us to an even larger, longer room. Some poles run along the middle, supporting the ceiling. Thick glass panels have been set in place along one side of the room, the side with small round windows in it. Panels also cover the far end of the room, where there's an access door. The result is a sealed, self-contained, L-shaped corridor.

The half-dozen members of the Board are standing on the other side of the glass, in the corridor. The Prince and Justin Bazini are puffing fat cigars. Lady Jemima is smoking a cigarette clasped in a long, fancy holder. Lord Luca pops a few pills. Vicky Wedge is leaning against the glass, breathing heavily, her arms crossed, and Dan-Dan is close by her, tapping on the glass with his fingers, cooing at me as if I was a caged bird. At one point he leans forward and licks the glass. Then he draws a little heart in his spit and flutters his eyelashes at me.

There are bloodstains smeared across the glass on my side. Bits of flesh are stuck to it in places. Bones are scattered across the floor.

'Can you hear us, little girl?' Dan-Dan calls. 'Is the sound system working? It had better be. I don't like it when that breaks down. Heads will roll if there are any technical problems today.'

'We can hear you loud and clear, Lord Wood,' Coley replies.

Dan-Dan smiles. 'I can hear you too. That's perfect.'

'Unbind her and come on round,' Justin says to Barnes and Coley. 'We want to share the show with you, a reward for all the hard work you've put in over the last few weeks.'

Barnes faces me. 'We can do this the hard way if you want. I can taser you and release you while you're subdued. But if you give me your word not to attack us, we can just take off the cuffs and leave you be.'

'No need for the taser,' I beam. 'I'll be a good girl. Promise.'

Barnes stares at me for a few beats, then grins tightly. 'I don't believe you.'

I drop the fake smile. 'That's because I'm lying. If I get the chance, I'll rip your throats open and wallow in your blood before you die.'

'You'd rather the taser?'

'Bring it on.'

Barnes sighs and gives Coley the nod. 'I'm loving

this,' Coley says, then lets me have it. I collapse in a spasming heap. Stars fill my head again. The agony is even worse than the first time and seems to last longer.

As I start to recover, I realise that my hands and legs are free. Coley and Barnes removed the cuffs and withdrew from the room while my senses were swimming. They're on the other side of the glass now, with the guys and gals of the Board. No guards in sight.

'This used to be the dining hall,' Dan-Dan tells me. He's pawing the glass, like a puppy waiting for a treat. 'The Wardroom was reserved for the officers. This was for the common crew. I prefer the informal atmosphere here. How about you?'

I try to tell him where he can stuff his *informal atmosphere*, but my mouth isn't working properly yet. All that comes out is a low mumbling noise.

'You haven't broken her, have you?' Dan-Dan snaps at Barnes and Coley. 'If you have, we'll kill her and send you straight out to find another one for us. I want a fully functional, talking zombie. I won't settle for second best.'

'She'll be fine in a minute or two,' Barnes assures him.

'She'd better be,' Dan-Dan growls. 'Poor thing. Did they hurt you, little girl? Don't worry, Dan-Dan will make the pain go away. I'd kiss you better if I could. Dan-Dan loves his clever zombie, yes he does.'

'Heaven save us from simpletons,' Lady Jemima sighs. 'Maybe we should throw Daniel in there with her.'

'Careful,' Lord Luca snarls. 'That's my brother you're talking about.'

'I was only joking,' Lady Jemima says quickly. 'I adore him really.'

As the would-be rulers of the world snipe at one another, the door to my side of the room opens and two guards step in and move to either side. They train their guns on me and tell me to take a few steps back. When I've retreated, a zombie is hustled in by another guard. There's a collar around the zombie's neck, attached to a stiff lead, giving the guard plenty of space.

Yet another guard enters, with a second captive

zombie, followed by three more. Then one last guard comes in. This guy's holding a taser like Coley's. He gives each zombie a quick burst. As they fall to the floor and writhe, their handlers set them free and slip out of the room. The pair with guns are the last to leave and they slam shut the door after themselves. While the zombies on the floor recover, I study them cautiously. Three men, a woman and a teenage boy. The men are muscular and dressed in normal clothes. The woman is wearing a chef's outfit. The boy is naked.

'I chose that one,' Dan-Dan sniggers. 'Nudity is so pleasing to the eye, isn't it, especially in one so young and pure?'

'You're a degenerate,' Lord Luca laughs.

'Not at all,' Dan Dan tuts. 'I simply like to appreciate the human form in all its natural glory.'

'An interesting mix,' Justin murmurs, then calls out to me. 'As the street-smart young woman that you appear to be, I'm sure you've already sussed the state of play. We want you to fight to the death. We've been pitting living slaves against zombies for months now, but they've struggled to stage an engaging fight. It seems the true gladiatorial spirit died out among the human masses long ago. But we're sure you'll serve up a decent show.'

I slide my jaw from side to side and wriggle my tongue about to make sure I can speak again. Then I shoot Justin the finger. 'Get stuffed, grandad.'

Justin shakes his head bitterly. 'Why do the youth of today have to make it so hard on themselves? Vicky, would you lend me your assistance?'

'My pleasure.' She moves to a small hatch which I hadn't noticed before. It's covered with a glass rectangle. She slides it open and draws a gun from a holster behind her back, kneels and aims at one of the male zombies.

'Fight or we'll kill him,' Justin says.

I shrug. 'You want me to kill him anyway, so what's the difference?'

'If you fight him, he stands a chance,' Justin says. 'And if he comes up short, at least he can die with honour.'

'I couldn't care less about honour,' I sniff.

'Do it,' Justin yaps and Vicky fires three times in quick succession. The man's head explodes and he slumps, truly dead now. The zombies around him snarl and dart at the hatch, angered by the attack and tempted by the scent of human brain. They slam into the glass but it barely quivers. Vicky shuts the hatch and moves to another—there are several of them set in the panels in different areas.

'Oh my God!' I scream, covering my ears with my hands. 'You did it! I didn't think you'd really do it!'

'We never bluff,' The Prince drawls, smiling as if he'd just won a war.

'Well, I don't either,' I jeer, lowering my hands and dropping the hysterical act. 'You lot are mugs. What do you think I am, zombie Spartacus or something? I don't give a toss about these walking corpses. Shoot them, fry them, chop them up into pieces if you want. I don't care.'

Justin frowns. 'You won't stand up to protect your own?'

'They're nothing to do with me,' I tell him. 'I don't have anything in common with these brain-dead abominations. Hell, I've finished off plenty of them myself over the last few months.'

'Interesting,' Justin murmurs. 'Then I suppose we'll have to try a different tack. Daniel, will you go and fetch us one of your darlings?'

'Yes, yes, yes, yes, yes!' Dan-Dan crows. 'I was hoping for this. But I want to be the one who does it if she forces our hand. They're mine. I won't let Vicky or any of the others cheat me out of my prize.'

'Perish the thought,' Justin says. 'The honour will be all yours.'

'In that case, I'll be back before you can blink.' Dan-Dan shoots out of the room as if in a hurry to get to a party.

'Is this really necessary?' The Prince asks with a pained look.

'Yes,' Justin says.

'It would have been so much simpler if you'd just fought when asked,' The Prince admonishes me.

'What's happening?' Coley asks Justin. 'Where did Lord Wood go?'

'To bring us something truly dreadful,' Justin whispers, his eyes dark and sad, yet bright and excited at the same time.

FOURTEEN

Dan-Dan returns several minutes later and my heart sinks. Or would, if I had one.

He has a couple of kids with him, and both of them are alive.

'These are my darlings,' Dan-Dan coos, rubbing their heads and pointing them towards me. 'Say hello, my dears.'

The children mumble a frightened hello. One is a boy, the other a girl. Neither is more than seven or eight years old. They're dressed in sailor suits similar to Dan-Dan's. The boy looks like he's been crying. The girl's eyes are dry but she's clearly scared. Both are trembling.

'What's going on?' Barnes asks sharply.

'Surely you must have heard the rumours back in the day about the child-killer Daniel Wood?' Justin chuckles.

'Children had a habit of meeting with an unfortunate end whenever Daniel came to town,' Vicky trills. 'He was such a naughty little boy.'

'My darlings,' Dan-Dan beams, hugging the children. 'They keep me company. I have nightmares when I'm by myself. My playmates help me keep body and soul together.'

'The trouble is, Daniel plays rough,' Lady Jemima notes, smiling cynically.

'He kills each child in the end, when he grows bored of them,' Justin grunts.

'Allegedly,' Lord Luca beams. 'Nothing was ever proven in a court of law. Why, he was never even prosecuted.'

Vicky Wedge winks at me. 'The advantage of having

an unholy amount of money, and associates like me in high places.'

'You never told me any of this before,' Barnes snaps.

'Why should we?' Justin yawns. 'You're hired help.' He turns his attention to me. 'Now, Becky Smith, you might not care about the dead, but what about the living? Will you fight or does Daniel have to start squeezing?'

Dan-Dan slides his arms up and locks them round the children's throats. The girl begins to cry. Dan-Dan smiles darkly.

'It's always sad when I have to bid a darling good-bye,' he croaks. 'I miss each and every one. I used to keep a list of their names, but it grew so long ...'

'You won't do it,' I say weakly.

'As I already told you, we never bluff,' The Prince murmurs but he sounds ashamed of his boast.

'Stop,' Barnes shouts. 'This is sick. I won't stand by and let you —'

'You will do what you're told!' Vicky Wedge screeches and aims her gun at him. Lord Luca, Lady

Jemima and The Prince draw weapons too. Coley curses and darts behind Barnes.

'Don't shoot!' Coley cries. 'I'm on your side!'

Barnes stands firm, eyes filled with fury and contempt.

Justin gazes serenely at Barnes. 'There's no need for the guns,' he says to the others. 'Our man Barnes is smarter than that. He knows there are guards outside. They are armed and he is not. If he threatened us, they would execute him. The children too.'

'This is wrong,' Barnes snarls. 'You can't use innocent children this way.'

'Of course we can,' Justin snorts. 'We make the laws. We can do anything we want.'

'If it's any comfort to you, they're orphans,' Lady Jemima says. 'We have them delivered from camps. We only pick those who have no one to worry about them. We're not complete monsters.'

'You always did have a soft heart, my lovely,' Justin murmurs and turns his back on the glaring but impotent Barnes. 'We're waiting for your answer, Becky.'

'He's going to kill them in the end anyway,' I say softly.

'Probably,' Justin nods. 'But there's always a chance that he will take pity on these two. Or they might escape.'

'Oh, they never escape,' Dan-Dan whispers.

'There are others,' Lord Luca says.

'Fourteen or fifteen the last time I checked,' Vicky purrs.

'If you don't please us, he'll kill this pair and fetch replacements,' The Prince adds glumly.

'He can be very petulant when he doesn't get his way,' Lady Jemima concludes.

Both children are trying to tear free of Dan-Dan's grip. They're old enough to know what's going on. Dan-Dan is sweating with delight, his muscles bulging. I think he wants me to defy him, so that he can kill openly, like a disgusting, spoilt brat who wants to show off his latest vile habit.

'If I do this,' I say hollowly, 'I want to see the children every day, the whole group, so I can be sure that he hasn't killed any of them.'

'Hold on a minute,' Dan-Dan yaps. 'You're in no position to make demands.'

'Yes she is,' Justin overrides him. 'Agreed.'

'No!' Dan-Dan howls. 'They're mine. I'll do what I want with them.'

'Not under *my* watch,' Justin says, features darkening. 'This isn't a democracy. The girl is something new, something different. If you have to stop killing for a few weeks or months, to entice her to play ball, so be it. You're not going to spoil things for the rest of us.'

'Luca . . .' Dan-Dan whines, looking to his brother for support.

Lord Luca shrugs. 'I'm with Justin this time. I'm bored of the same old pathetic show, humans failing miserably every time we stick them in with the undead. I crave savage duels, heated action, true drama. If the girl has a reason to battle on – if she's fighting for others, not just herself – it will be all the more interesting.'

'You can have your darlings eventually,' Vicky says soothingly. 'We're not taking them away from you forever. You just need to be patient.'

'Oh, very well,' Dan-Dan pouts, releasing the children and pushing them aside. 'But I won't forget this. The next time one of you asks for a favour, don't expect me to jump.'

The Prince gathers the children from Dan-Dan and escorts them to the door, where he passes them to a guard who takes them back to their quarters.

'You can leave as well if you wish,' Justin says to Barnes. 'I won't make you watch if it offends you. This was meant to be a reward for services rendered, not a punishment.'

Barnes studies the businessman, stares at the open doorway, then looks back at me and shrugs. 'I was only worried about the kids. Now that we've dealt with that issue, I'm keen to stick around.'

'Excellent,' Justin beams. 'Becky, can you agitate them by yourself or do you need some help?'

'I've got it,' I mutter, flexing my fingers and preparing for battle.

I let my gaze linger on the undead men and woman for a moment, then stare glumly at the teenage boy. They're all standing with their backs to me, trying to gouge through the glass, unaware of the threat behind them. It would be easy to step up and drive my hands through their skulls, kill them all before they could react. But that wouldn't satisfy the bloodthirsty members of the Board. They want action and excitement, and it's my job to deliver that for them.

'Mum would be proud,' I snort. 'She always wanted me to go into showbiz.' Then, to cheers of encouragement from the inhuman humans, I sweep forward and attack.

FIFTEEN

I grab the collars of the men's shirts and haul them away from the glass. I kick the boy in the chest and send him sprawling. I slap the woman's face.

The zombies snarl and regroup. They stare at me, sniffing the air. They know I'm undead, so they're not sure why I've assaulted them. Zombies don't turn on one another. They find the peaceful unity in death that is so rare in life.

'Come on,' I growl, crooking my fingers at them. 'I'm not as dead as I look.'

They hiss and move closer, then stall and stare

again. They can tell I'm not the same as them – no regular zombie can talk – but I'm more like them than the humans. They're reluctant to strike, seeing me as one of their own.

'Don't just stand there,' Dan-Dan calls, banging his fist on the glass. 'Make them angry.'

I give him the finger, then dart forward. I kick the boy in the chest again and scratch the cheek of the nearest man. He instinctively throws a fist at me. I block it and punch him hard in the stomach.

The woman in the chef's outfit grabs my head and shakes it, pulling me away from the men. The boy leaps at me, growling like a dog. I kick him between the legs. Because he's naked, I have a clear shot. Every guy on the other side of the glass gasps and cringes. Then they cheer and clap.

I shrug off the woman and race towards a nearby pole. The men follow. I jump into the air, grab the pole and whirl around. I stick my legs out and my right foot connects with one of the men's jaw. His head snaps back and he staggers away.

'Oh, nice shot,' The Prince applauds. 'We never saw any of the others execute a move like that.'

'It's like watching a wrestling match,' Lady Jemima cackles.

'Only the result isn't fixed,' Justin laughs.

I tune out the babbling members of the Board and stay focused. Any one of these zombies could slice my skull open. I can't afford to get cocky.

The boy shambles towards me, still grimacing from the kick between his legs. I hate doing this to him, but the shot is there to be taken, so I swing my foot back, then kick him square in the nuts again.

'Unbelievable!' Lord Luca hoots.

'He'll be a eunuch by the end of this,' Vicky Wedge sniggers.

'It's bringing tears to my eyes,' Dan-Dan squeals, crossing his hands in front of his groin.

One of the men tackles me from behind and locks his arms across my chest. The other man charges me from the front. I lift my legs, clasp them around his neck in a scissor motion and snap it. He groans and wheels away, tugging at his head, trying to set it straight.

The man behind me squeezes, but there's no air in my lungs, so he doesn't do much damage. While he's trying to suffocate me, I twist my body the way I was trained by Master Zhang and throw him over my shoulder. He lands heavily in front of me. I make a blade of my fingers and drive my right hand through the centre of his forehead. He cries out, shudders, then falls still. I withdraw my hand and wipe it across his hair, cleaning my flesh of bits of the dead man's brain.

The woman slashes at me with the bones sticking out of her fingers. I block them with my own fingerbones, then jab at her eyes, forcing her back.

The boy lurches at me from the other side. He still hasn't properly protected his crown jewels, but I'm not able to find the angle to kick him a third time. He grabs me and digs his teeth into my left hip, tearing through my trousers, into the flesh.

I wince and club the boy over the head. His skull snaps and some of the flesh tears open. I spot brain

and swiftly dig in, finishing him off. After the blows to his wedding tackle, I think death comes as a relative blessing.

The woman hurls herself at me, shrieking. For all I know, she was the boy's mother in life. Not that I think that factors into things now. She only wants to kill the beast who is threatening her. Zombies can't feel love, pity or affection. But they can feel fear. How unfair is that?

I shimmy out of the woman's way, slip in behind and get her in a stranglehold. She struggles furiously, but I was taught how to keep my grip tight. As she reels around the room with me on her back, I bare my fangs and bite into her skull. I chew loose a chunk of flesh and bone, and spit it out. I bite again. The woman mewls and shudders. After I tear away another chunk, there's enough space for me to jam in my chin, like a pig sticking its snout into a trough. I munch, rip and saw.

Seconds later the woman collapses beneath me and I push myself to my feet, spitting out brain. The brains of the undead do nothing for me. The taste is vile, nothing like the juicy, enticing brains of the living.

The only one left is the man with the broken neck. He doesn't provide much resistance. He's still trying to repair the damage to his spinal cord. I simply have to pad up behind him and crack his head open.

I step away from the last of the corpses and gaze at my handiwork. Four dead zombies, in addition to the one Vicky killed. It probably didn't take me more than a couple of minutes to fell them.

The members of the Board are cheering warmly. I glance at them numbly, blood on my hands, brains dribbling from my lips. The Prince winks at me. Lord Luca gives me the thumbs up. Justin claps louder than the others and shouts over the noise, 'Ladies and gentlemen, a gladiator is born!'

The nightmare begins for real.

SIXTEEN

It's been a week or more since I wound up in the clutches of the Board. A week of almost non-stop fighting, with rests only to allow my captors to sleep, eat and indulge in their other pastimes.

When I'm not needed, I'm kept in a room near the fore of the cruiser, in what used to be known as a mess. A few hammocks are slung across it. I lie in one of those when I'm relaxing, sometimes for hours without moving, staring at the ceiling with my unblinking eyes, trying to think of a way out of this horror show.

In an ideal world I'd kill the creeps of the Board, free the children and slip away into the night. Since I'm unlikely to score on all three fronts, I'd settle for murdering the manipulative monsters who think they're superior to the rest of us.

But there's not much chance of that. They keep themselves separate. I usually only see them in the converted dining hall when they want me to kill. And then they're always safe behind their wall of glass. Many of my opponents have tried to smash through that wall. I've even thrown a few of them at it with all my strength while fighting, to test it. Not so much as a crack. It's tough as steel.

The battles have drained me. Zombies are more resilient than humans, but we're not inexhaustible. We wear down. I've fought four or five times most days, usually against a handful of opponents, but sometimes as many as eight. I'm not stronger than those I've come up against, but I'm sharper. I can outwit and outmanoeuvre them.

Even so, I've suffered my share of injuries. I've broken several bones. My neck and chest have been slashed, chunks bitten out of my arms and legs. A couple of teeth were smashed from my gums—that *really* hurt and still does.

Justin spoke of keeping me on for months when I first arrived, but I'll be lucky to last a fortnight, maybe a bit longer if they reduce the number of daily bouts. I'm a short-term project for them.

I wasn't going to tell them that I need brains to function, that I'll regress if I don't eat. But they know that zombies need to feed to stay sharp, so they supplied me with brains without my having to ask for them, a couple of days after I'd fallen into their foul clutches. Coley delivered the first batch.

'Barnes and I rustled these up from corpses on the streets,' he told me. 'Not my idea of a good time, but anything to please our lords and ladies.'

'What if I don't want to eat?' I said in a low voice.

Coley shrugged. 'They'll see that as a sign of mutiny and give me the order to put you out of your misery. Which is fine by me, so go ahead and refuse.'

I made a sighing noise and dug in. I wouldn't have been able to resist for long anyway, not once the brains had been set before me. I'd seen it in the zom heads when they were starved. As you approach the end of consciousness, you lose control. In a few days I'd have dug into the brains regardless.

'Dan-Dan didn't want us to go foraging for used brains,' Coley said as I threw up the remains of the brains once I'd absorbed the nutrients from them. 'He had a more novel idea. He wanted to put one of the guards in with you, make you kill him and eat his fresh brain. He's some piece of work, isn't he? Makes Barnes and me look like a pair of saints. You didn't know how lucky you were when we were the worst you had to deal with.'

Coley got that much right. Dan-Dan is a real beauty, full of unpleasant ideas. He came to see me the day after my first fight. Six guards flanked him and he kept well back. He wanted me to wear a revealing leather outfit, the sort you used to find in seedy adult shops.

'Not a hope in hell,' I told him.

'I'll kill one of my darlings if you don't wear it,' he huffed.

'That threat won't work this time,' I dismissed him. 'I'll tell Justin and refuse to fight in protest. The others wouldn't like that, would they?'

'You're no fun,' Dan-Dan pouted, then slunk away like the disgusting rat that he is.

Even given my functioning brain, I'd have come unstuck long before now if not for my training. Master Zhang taught me well. I zing around that room like a pinball, striking swiftly, slipping out of reach before my foes can counter. I'm improving all the time, learning new tricks, finding a whole string of ways to attack and defend. I'd be proud of how I've performed if I wasn't so sickened by what is being asked of me.

The living dead deserve better than this. I don't have a lot of sympathy for zombies. They're killers by nature. But they didn't ask for reanimation or the hunger that drives them. They're not responsible for their actions. The rest of us, on the other hand, are. And what we're doing here is disgraceful. Sure, I've killed reviveds before, like in the tunnel under Waterloo Station, but that was to prepare for a battle with evil. It wasn't for sport.

I tried wriggling off the hook a couple of days ago. I carefully dropped my guard while fighting, moved a bit slower than I could, let myself be pummelled. That's when I lost the teeth. I'd planned to lose a whole lot more, to let my opponents carve me up. But Vicky got wise to what I was plotting.

'You can do better than that, Miss Smith,' she called out as I circled three undead guys, each double the size of me.

'Why don't you come in and try if you think it's that easy?' I snarled.

'That will not be necessary,' she retaliated. 'I can see what you're up to. The stench of treachery is thick in the air. You want out. Rest assured, if you are defeated today, every one of Dan-Dan's darlings will be executed within the hour. And it will not be swift or painless.'

I cursed Vicky Wedge and the rest of them, but they had me by the short and curlies. There was nothing for it but to up my game and fight for real. I came out the undefeated champion, but the victory cost me dear. I've been hobbling in pain ever since.

The door to my room opens and I raise myself, groaning, ready to fight again. But no guards enter this time. Instead it's Barnes. I haven't seen him since that day when I was first presented to the Board.

'Come to gloat?' I snarl, letting myself fall back into my hammock.

'No,' he says, taking a seat. I'm not chained up, so I could attack him, but he doesn't look afraid. Either he's sure I'll leave him be out of fear of reprisal, or he's confident that he could draw his gun and open fire before I got my hands on him.

'Come to take my order then? Cool. I'll have my brains fried, sunny side up.'

Barnes grins. 'I'll pass your request on to Coley.'

'Where is your trusty sidekick?' I ask.

'Taking it easy. Having some fun.'

'I thought he might be cowering behind you again.'

Barnes chuckles. 'That wasn't his finest moment. I haven't brought it up with him yet, but I certainly plan to. I'm just waiting for the right time.'

'This is all screwed,' I mutter. 'I don't care what

these guys are doing for you, nothing can justify this. You've sided with a pack of demons. Dan-Dan torments and kills children. How can you live with yourself, serving a beast like that?'

'I don't have to explain my motives to the likes of you,' Barnes grunts. 'You killed plenty of kids yourself, I'm sure, when you turned.'

'That's different. I couldn't control myself. I can now. You can too. But you choose not to.'

'Our choices are sometimes limited,' Barnes sighs, then shakes his head and squints at me. 'Enough of the soul-baring. I'm here to offer you a deal.'

'This should be interesting,' I sneer.

'You've lost your sheen,' Barnes says. 'You're slowing up. The constant fighting has taken it out of you. You're slow to heal – if you heal at all – and your wounds are weakening you. Our lords and ladies have started to worry. They enjoy watching you in action. They don't want to lose their prize plaything.'

'Tell them if they love me, they should set me free,' I say sweetly.

Barnes laughs. 'I like you, Becky, I truly do. You've

got more balls than most of the guys I've ever known. I want to help you if I can.'

I cock an eyebrow at the hunter. 'If you're looking to break me out, I'm all ears.'

Barnes smiles wryly. 'I don't like you *that* much. But I've come up with a compromise that might work. The Board want me to find other zombies like you, who can speak and think. They want to see you take on one of your own, someone who can mount a genuine challenge. They've instructed me to find a few of your friends, like the ones I saw you with in Leicester Square.'

I flash my teeth at him. 'I don't have any *friends*.'

'Then you won't mind if I find some of the gang you were with, bring them back here and force you to fight them,' he says calmly.

I glare at him and don't respond.

'*Or,*' Barnes says teasingly, 'we can strike a deal.'

'What's this deal you keep going on about?' I sniff.

'Simple,' he says. 'Tell me where your colleagues are. I'll round up the lot of them. Then we'll set you free.'

I smother a laugh. 'You expect me to believe you'd let me go?'

'I'm not a liar.'

'But you're also not the main man here. Not even close. The lords and ladies of the Board would never sanction my release.'

'They already have,' Barnes says. 'I took the offer to them before I came to you. Said I didn't think you'd go for it, but that I wanted to know where they stood if you did. They voted four to two in your favour. I won't tell you who voted against you, as I'd hate to sour the special relationship you have with them.'

'What makes you think they'd honour their pledge?' I ask.

'Easier to do that than betray me. They might not think much of me as a man, but they respect me as a soldier. Besides, I'm useful to them. There will be other ways I can help them further down the line. You have my guarantee that we'll make good on our promise.'

I don't really have to think about it, but I give

myself a minute to mull it over, just to be absolutely sure of my answer. When I've decided, I smirk and rock in my hammock. 'Sorry, Barnes. Couldn't help you even if I wanted. Like I told the Board, we moved around all the time. We don't have a base. I've no idea where they might be.'

Barnes nods and stands. 'I expected nothing more but felt I owed you the offer. I'll find them anyway. Hunting's what I excel at. I'll track them down, subdue them and drag their sorry asses back here.

'I hope those conscious zombies truly aren't your friends. Because soon you're going to have to face them in the arena and kill or be killed. And there's nothing worse than having to sacrifice someone you care about. Take it from one who knows.'

On that enigmatic note he leaves and, as I carry on rocking, I reflect bitterly on the fact that my future, as short as it was already given my dire situation, probably just got a hell of a lot shorter.

SEVENTEEN

I'm marched down to see the children every day. They're being held on the deck beneath mine. They sleep in bunk beds. The boiler room is nearby and that's where they play and exercise. I usually view them there. They're pale from lack of sunlight and haggard-looking, but they seem to be enjoying their respite and have been a bit cheerier every day.

There are fifteen of them, mostly boys, but some girls too. I never get to spend a lot of time with them and we don't talk much. But at least I can see that they're alive and being taken care of. For however long I might last.

It's been nine or ten days since Barnes made his offer. Part of me wishes I'd accepted. I was telling the truth when I said I didn't have any friends among the Angels. That was the advantage of keeping my distance. I could have sold them out, walked away a free girl, put this episode behind me and tried to forget about the Board and my treachery.

But, as bad as things get, I never really regret telling Barnes to get stuffed. I don't want to see out the rest of my days as a Judas, especially given the fact that I might live for a few thousand years. There are some things you can never forget or forgive yourself for.

Mind you, I won't have to worry about thousands of years in my current state. I've taken several severe hammerings over the last week. I'm getting sluggish. I can't move as swiftly as I did, or react as sharply as I could at my peak. I'm running on willpower alone these days. If it wasn't for the children, I'd give up the ghost. But I've got to buy them as much time as I can. A few days won't make any difference to me, but it might to them.

I watch the children running round the boiler room, smiling softly to myself as they play hide-and-seek. I wish the guards would leave me here for an hour or two, but they never allow me more than a few minutes, just enough time to do a headcount and satisfy myself that they're all as well as they can be given the wretched circumstances.

'Aren't they wonderful?' someone murmurs behind me.

I glance over my shoulder and my smile disappears. It's Dan-Dan. He's wearing a fireman's outfit today. It doesn't fit him any better than his sailor's costume.

'Why don't you get clothes the right size?' I growl. 'Nobody wants to look at your belly.'

'*I* like looking at it,' he giggles. 'And I like my tight clothes. They feel much better when they're cutting into me.'

He moves forward, careful not to get too close. My arms are tied behind my back and my ankles are shackled together, but I still pose a threat and Dan-Dan is all too aware of it. Keeping a safe distance, he stops at a railing and studies the children.

'I miss them so much,' he sighs. 'You have no idea how lonely and scared I get when I'm by myself. I never have nightmares when I torture and kill. And the nightmares are so terrifying . . .'

'Stop,' I whimper. 'You'll make me cry.'

'I don't expect you to understand,' he says. 'Hardly anyone does. All I can tell you is that I bitterly regret the day I let you convince me to stop killing in order to watch you fight. The fighting bores me now.'

'It doesn't bore the others,' I note.

'Not yet,' he concedes. 'But their interest will wane soon, as mine has. They'll discard you like a dull blade once Barnes returns with fresh, intelligent zombies. Even if he can't find any, I don't think you'll enjoy their favour much longer. They're tired of your face. Nobody likes watching the same person triumph all the time. We only endure your victories because they'll make your ultimate defeat so much sweeter when it comes.'

'Maybe I won't lose. Maybe I'll win every time, go on for years. What do you think of that, Fireman Dan?'

Dan-Dan shakes his head and smirks. 'We can all see that you're close to the end. It's been fascinating, watching your energy ebb away. Educational too. We never knew a zombie could be worn down like one of the living. We've learnt a lot by studying you. I think we'll push your replacements less strenuously, make them last longer.'

Dan-Dan turns and stands with his back to the railing. 'By the way, they won't let you die in the arena. When you reach the stage where you can't fight any longer, they're going to hand you over to me.'

'What are you talking about?' I snap.

'I told them I couldn't bear it,' he giggles. 'Said I was going mad, not being able to kill. I demanded access to my darlings. To keep me quiet, they've offered you to me instead of the children. When you run out of steam, the guards will drag you out of there before you're killed. They'll tie you up neatly and deliver you to my personal quarters. I have so many things I want to share with you before the end.'

'You won't get your filthy hands on me,' I snarl. 'I'll let the zombies kill me first.'

'You think so?' Dan-Dan grins. 'It won't be easy. If they could slit your throat open and finish you off that way, you might stand a chance. But they have to dig through your skull and tear out your brain, chunk by chunky chunk. That takes time. We'll shoot them before they rip you apart. Vicky and Luca will save you. For me.'

Dan-Dan's grin fades and he takes a step closer. 'You probably think you know pain intimately. But let me tell you, little girl, you don't. I'm going to put you through a whole new universe of torment before I grant you blessed release. I'm in no rush, and you can take so much more than any of my darlings. I might keep you writhing around on a leash for weeks. Imagine that, weeks of delirious suffering, where every moment is agony redefined and writ large.'

'Screw you,' I moan.

Dan-Dan smiles again. 'No,' he says breezily. 'You're the one who's screwed. I'm looking forward to working with you more closely, Becky. You will be my masterpiece. The one to whom I reveal the true, unfathomable depths of my twisted fury. When I set to work on you, the results might shock even me.

'Toodle-pip!'

With a sick chuckle, he slides past and exits, leaving me in the boiler room with his darlings. Their excited cries as they search for each other don't sound quite so cheery now. In fact they sound eerily like the screams of the damned.

EIGHTEEN

I'm led into the arena for another gruelling bout. I keep hoping that the guards will grow careless. I've gone along with them meekly each time, acting as if my spirits have been crushed, obeying their every command, eager to please. Praying that they might stop regarding me as a threat. All I need is a small slip, a glimmer of a chance.

But so far they've followed their guidelines impeccably. They truss me up expertly, slip a collar round my neck and check the steel lead a few times before forcing me out of the mess. There are always extra guards around, guns cocked and aimed, ready to cut me down if I revolt.

'Here's our girl,' Dan-Dan chortles as I'm guided in. He's back in his sailor's costume. The other zombies are already in place, still held captive by their guards. They always release us at the same time, so they can exit together.

'How have you been, my dear?' Lady Jemima asks, faking concern. 'You were struck a nasty blow last time. We were worried about you.'

'I'm fine,' I mutter, trying to ignore the throbbing at the back of my head where I was clubbed in my previous fight.

'You don't look too lively,' Justin says critically. 'Perhaps you'd like to sit this one out? We can send you back to the mess if you'd prefer.'

I'd love a good rest but I'm wary. I don't think I'll be returned to the mess if they judge me too weary to fight. Once they reckon I've run out of steam, I figure I'll be delivered straight to Dan-Dan's quarters.

'Nothing wrong with me,' I sniff. 'I'm all fired up and raring to go.'

'Very well,' Justin smiles. 'Release the beasts.'

Our handlers taser us, set us free and retreat. Once I've recovered from the shock, I roll my arms around, limbering up, and check out my latest batch of opponents as they surge towards the glass and paw at the panels, trying to break through to the six smug humans on the other side.

There are seven zombies, five men and two women. Each looks like they had plenty of experience of fighting when they were alive. One of the women is wearing a karate outfit. She must have been training or taking part in a competition when she was attacked.

I've faced all sorts of opponents here, but most have been bruisers like this lot, especially in recent battles. The Board are pushing me to my limits, waiting for me to break.

'I bet she comes undone this time,' Lady Jemima says as she studies the muscles on the two zombies closest to her.

'How much?' The Prince asks.

'This,' she says, flashing a diamond ring at him.

'Nice.' The Prince whistles. 'If you throw in the rest of the rings on that hand, I'll wager my crown.'

'Done,' Lady Jemima smirks.

'I didn't think you would risk so treasured a possession,' Vicky Wedge notes.

The Prince shrugs. 'There will be plenty of crowns to choose from when the world is ours.'

I decide to get things under way. I move forward wearily and make a nuisance of myself, angering the zombies, luring them away from the glass, focusing their attention on me.

We begin our waltz of death. Once they're riled up, I manipulate every last section of the arena, buzzing around like a fly, grabbing poles and whipping myself into the air, utilising the walls and ceiling as much as the floor. I know this area inside out and I use that knowledge to my advantage.

I jump and grab hold of one of the overhead pipes as two of the men charge towards me. From that position I can lash out at both of them at the same time with my feet.

A couple of poles are set close together in one zone. I grab the woman in the karate outfit and propel her towards them, then angle her head down and ram it between the poles, jamming her in place. I leave her there, stuck, to finish off at the end when I'm done with the others.

I barge one of the men into a wall at a point which I've identified as a possible weak spot. The steel panel always shakes when someone is thrown against it. I keep hoping that it will tear loose completely one day, but no joy so far. Today it rattles as usual but holds.

The members of the Board keep up a running commentary. They're sipping champagne, casually discussing the battle, their plans for the future, what they fancy for dinner. They're a boring, self-obsessed lot. I'd rather total silence, but I can't tell them that or they'd talk all the louder just to spite me.

The other female zombie snags the hole in my chest with her fingerbones and tears five nasty channels through the flesh down towards my belly button.

'Yowzers!' Dan-Dan howls happily as I roar with pain.

'That's got to hurt,' Lord Luca chuckles.

I kick the woman away and flee to the far side of the arena, gritting my teeth. I quickly examine the wounds to make sure no guts are spilling out. Then I leap over the head of one of the onrushing men. But I don't get as much height as I thought I would. He clips my legs and drags me to the ground, then bellows and smashes a fist at my face. The bones jutting out of his fingers glint in the light. If he connects, it's game over and at least I won't have to worry about ending up in the clutches of Dan-Dan.

But it's impossible to lie still and let myself be killed. My defences kick in automatically. I knock the man's hand aside and twist my head in the opposite direction. His fist slams into the floor and instead of breaking my skull, he breaks a few of the bones in his fingers.

I scramble to my feet and stagger away from the other reviveds, who are all closing in on me, except for the trapped woman. A long strip of ducting runs the length of what was once the dining hall. I jump and haul myself up, wedging myself between the ducting and the ceiling. There's just enough space for me. I've squeezed in here before when I've needed a rest.

The zombies punch the base and sides of the ducting, trying to grab hold and pull me down. But they can't get at me, except to scratch the sides of my arms and legs. If a few of them climbed up, the ducting would come crashing to the floor, leaving me at the mercy of my foes. But thankfully they aren't smart enough to work that out.

'No fair,' Dan-Dan shouts, slapping the glass. 'I hate it when she does that. Why can't we take that ducting out of there?'

'Now now,' Justin tuts. 'We have to give her a reasonable chance. It's more fun this way. She can't stay up there forever.'

I've tried crawling through the ducting at either end, but both exits have been sealed. Still, when I'm up here, I usually creep to one end or the other to hurl a few blows at the bolted-on steel plates, just in case there's any give.

I start pulling myself along like an injured snake. The zombies follow beneath me, scraping at the ducting, gurgling furiously. I wonder if they hate me more than the humans, if they see me as a traitor to the undead cause.

As I'm mulling that over and trying to tune out Dan-Dan's jeers, the sound of gunfire echoes down from the deck above. Nobody takes any notice of it at first. The guards on the upper deck often fire at passing zombies, or even at corpses floating down the river, for practice. But this time it doesn't stop after a few seconds as it normally does. It's sustained. Then, moments later, mingled in with the gunfire, I hear what might just be the sweetest noise ever.

Human screams.

The lords and ladies of the Board have fallen silent. They're staring at the open doorway on their side of the glass divide, heads cocked, jaws slack. They don't look like the masters and mistresses of the universe any more.

The zombies keep slapping at the ducting, unaware of the change of play. I ignore them and stare at the doorway along with the living.

A guard spills into the narrow corridor, falls over, then clambers to his feet. His face is contorted with terror. 'We're under attack!' he shouts.

'Who the hell dares attack us?' Justin barks, recovering his power of speech. 'Is it the army?'

The guard shakes his head. 'Zombies, I think. But we're not sure. They came from the river. They've swarmed the deck. I don't think we can hold for long.'

Justin curses foully, then draws a gun and shoots the startled guard through the middle of his forehead.

'Why did you do that?' The Prince shrieks.

'I don't spare messengers when they bring bad news,' Justin growls, then hops over the dead guard and into the corridor beyond.

The Prince stares at the corpse. There's another extended blast of gunfire overhead. He flinches, then hurries after Justin. Vicky, Lord Luca and Dan-Dan scramble after the first pair of deserters. Lady Jemima just sinks to the floor and covers her head with her hands. She starts moaning, 'No, no, no. This wasn't part of the plan. It can't happen like this. I won't let it. This is *our* world.'

Dan-Dan pauses in the doorway as the others flee. He looks back at me. I'm stunned to see him smirking. 'Isn't this exciting?' he coos.

'Run, run as fast you can, fat boy,' I snarl. 'But it won't make any difference. You're history.'

Dan-Dan snorts. 'I think not, little girl. I have more lives than a cat. See you later, alligator.'

'It'll be sooner than you'd like, crocodile.'

Dan-Dan winks. 'I'll be looking forward to the day.'

He skips out, laughing, leaving me to fend off the zombies and wait for whoever or whatever is coming.

NINETEEN

My gut instinct is that Mr Dowling and his mutants are orchestrating the attack. They set me free from prison once before when all seemed lost, and came to my rescue in Leicester Square when it looked like my goose was cooked. They're making a habit of saving my sorry neck from the chop. Long may it continue! I just hope they don't decide to kill me this time. Mr Dowling has shown mercy previously for some unknowable reason, but there's no telling which way the demented clown will blow when the wind changes direction.

I hang tight to the ducting and wait for the mutants or their master to find me. I'm hoping creepy Owl Man isn't with them. Then the door opens and a familiar figure bursts into the room and I realise my gut was just about as wrong as wrong can be.

'*Rage!*' I yell, for once with delight instead of contempt.

Rage squints at me. 'What are you doing up there?'

'This is what I do for kicks,' I growl. 'Now quit gawping and help me, will you?'

'Wait a minute,' Rage says and steps outside. 'She's here,' he hollers, then returns and lays into the zombies.

As Rage shoves the zombies away from me and starts cracking their heads open, Dr Oystein comes running into the room. 'B!' he cries, hurrying to where I'm hanging. He offers me his hand and helps me down.

'Nice to see you, doc,' I mutter.

'You too,' he says politely, then embraces me with

a surprisingly strong bear hug. 'I thought we had lost you forever.'

'You don't get rid of me that easily,' I chuckle, and hug him in return, burying my face in his chest, wishing I could cry so that I could blink back tears.

The twins race into the room as Dr Oystein releases me. They're dripping wet but they look ecstatic.

'We've taken control of the deck,' Cian cheers.

'Some of the guards are still fighting, but we have them trapped,' Awnya says.

'Master Zhang has started a sweep of the lower decks,' Cian adds. 'He says you should be cautious until he is certain the ship is ours.'

'There are children on the deck below this,' I tell the twins. 'Make sure nobody hurts them. They were being held captive.'

'We know all about the children,' Dr Oystein calms me. 'We will take good care of them and escort them back to County Hall when we have concluded our business here.'

'How did you find me?' I ask. 'How did you board the ship? Where –'

A scream stops me short. I look up. An Angel has entered the viewing area on the other side of the glass. It's Ingrid, the Angel I went on my very first ever mission with. Lady Jemima is backing away from her, eyes wide, shaking her head wildly.

'Who's this?' Ingrid asks me.

'A bitch who needs putting down,' I growl.

'Glad to be of service,' Ingrid grunts and closes in on the whimpering Lady Jemima. The human shuts her eyes and starts to pray, but why would God heed the prayers of a she-devil? Moments later it's all over as far as Lady J is concerned.

I push myself away from Dr Oystein. 'There were five others. They dressed differently to the guards. Have you seen them?'

'I saw one on the deck,' Dr Oystein replies. 'He was dressed like a prince. He tried to make the gangway. He did not get very far.'

'I spotted a few heading down the stairs,' Rage

says, pausing to address me over the heads of the zombies. 'One was dressed like a sailor.'

'*Dan-Dan,*' I growl and start for the door.

'B,' Dr Oystein calls me back. 'There are plenty of us onboard. We can handle this. You look drained and battered. You should rest.'

'I'll rest when those bastards are dead.' I grimace and flash the doc an apologetic smile. 'Sorry. I didn't mean to snap. But I need to do this. I want to make them pay for what they did to me.'

'I understand,' the doctor says, returning my smile. 'Good luck, B.'

'If you wait a minute, I can come with you,' Rage says, knocking another of the zombies to the floor.

'You're fine,' I tell him. 'This is something I'd rather do by myself.'

'Always the loner,' Rage laughs, bashing the heads of two more zombies together.

I want to respond to that but there isn't time. I'm worried that Dan-Dan and the rest of them might slip the net. Waving briefly to the doc and Rage, I slide out of the arena, a free girl for the first time since I came to this stinking cruiser, and head off in search of my captors. The tables have turned and I plan to put them through a whole heap of hurt before I break their rotten necks and rid this world of their unholy, stinking presence.

TWENTY

I hurry to the nearest set of stairs and practically throw myself down to the deck beneath. I pause and sniff the air. I can smell the children but no one from the Board. Of course my nose isn't infallible. If they raced fore or aft, I wouldn't be able to sniff them out from here. But I'm guessing they delved further into the bowels of the ship.

I carry on down to the next level. Gunfire starts afresh as I'm looking around. Screams. Master Zhang and his Angels must have found more guards. If the members of the Board are with them, they're finished. I just have to hope that they pressed on. If not, I'll find their corpses later and vomit over them to demonstrate my disgust.

Down another flight of stairs. The engine room is on this floor. I can't smell anything, but as I'm standing at the base of the stairs, weighing up my options, I hear a clanging noise. I move ahead cautiously, not getting my hopes up. There are all sorts of people on the old cruiser, crew members, guards, zombies, Angels. There's no guarantee that one of the louses of the Board made the noise.

More gunfire overhead helps mask the sound of my footsteps. I come to the engine room and let myself in. The place is filled with banks of dials and switches. I've no idea what any of them do and I don't care. All that matters to me is the smell in the air, familiar and sweet the closer I draw.

I hear them before I see them. Lord Luca is muttering angrily. 'I told you we should have stuck with Justin and Vicky. It was madness branching off on our own.'

'They're the mad ones,' Dan-Dan replies merrily, as if he hadn't a care in the world. 'It was crazy, pushing on. We don't know how fast the zombies can move. I wouldn't want to get into a race with them. Better to get out of here as swiftly as we can.'

'But how?' Lord Luca shouts. 'I don't know which button we're supposed to press. I wasn't paying attention when they showed us. There were so many escape routes and options, I can't remember them all.'

'You never did have the keenest attention span,' Dan-Dan laughs.

'I don't see you doing any better, genius,' Lord Luca snaps.

I round a bank of dials and come in view of the pair. Lord Luca is standing before a wall of switches, desperately flicking every one that he can. Dan-Dan is standing behind him, giggling.

'Having fun, boys?' I murmur.

Their heads snap round. Lord Luca yelps and throws switches faster than before. Dan-Dan tips his hat at me and says, 'I didn't expect you to catch up with me this quickly.'

'I don't believe in wasting time,' I grin, taking a step towards them, savouring the moment, wanting to make it last.

'We can pay you!' Lord Luca shrieks. 'We'll give you anything you want!'

'There's only one thing she wants,' Dan-Dan chuckles, then grabs his brother by the arm and spins him towards me.

'No!' Lord Luca cries as he crashes to the floor in front of me. 'What are you doing? Help me, fool!'

'You're the fool,' Dan-Dan gurgles, rubbing his hairy belly, picking a crumb from it and placing it delicately on his outstretched tongue. 'I never did like you, Luca. You were weak and scatterbrained like Mother. Father always said he only kept you around in case he ever needed an organ transplant. Poor Papa was always worried about his kidneys and heart.'

Lord Luca gawps with disbelief at his grotesque brother, then gulps and stares up at me. His look of fear fades, to be replaced by one of calm resignation. 'Is there any point begging for mercy?' he asks.

'No,' I tell him, then grab the sides of his head and lower my mouth. I lick his forehead and rub my nose across it. He whimpers, fear creeping back across his expression again. Then I bite into his skull and gnaw through the bone into the brain beneath. I'd like to make it last longer, but I'm anxious to move on to Dan-Dan.

When Lord Luca stops moaning and struggling, I let his body drop and face Dan-Dan, wiping bits of his brother's brain from my lips. To my surprise, the child-killer is crying.

'It's silly, isn't it?' Dan-Dan weeps. 'I cried when Mother died too, even though I threw her to the zombies, just as I've thrown Luca to you. I'm too soft for this cruel world.'

'You won't have to worry about it for much longer,' I chuckle grimly.

He squints at me. 'You really are a beautifully fearsome creature. I'm sorry I didn't get a chance to go to

work on you. There's so much more to you than any of my darlings. The sweet torments I could have put you through ...'

'Sorry to disappoint you,' I hiss.

'No need to apologise,' he smiles. 'You were simply doing what you had to. I don't hold it against you. I'm not one to bear a grudge.'

'Well, the bad news is, I am.' I flex my fingers and advance. 'I'm gonna hurt you, Dan-Dan. It won't be quick like it was for Luca. You promised me a universe of pain. Well, you're gonna reap what you planned to sow. For what you did to me and the children, I'm going to make it long and slow and painful.'

Dan-Dan shakes his head. 'I don't think so. You might want to torture me but you haven't the stomach for it. Few people have. I'm gifted. Emotions never got between me and my desires. I've always had the power to do whatever I wished.

'I'm going to miss you, Becky,' he says. 'What I wouldn't give to pinch your clammy cheek and kiss you goodnight as I put you to sleep forever. That time will come, I'm sure, but the days will be long and lonely without you until then.'

'Don't worry,' I tell him. 'You'll have plenty of company in Hell while you're waiting for me.'

'Oh, I'm not going to Hell just yet,' Dan-Dan says brightly. 'My brother was feather-headed. I was toying with him before you arrived. I wanted him to sweat. I always loved to wind up Luca. But I have a very good memory and I pay attention to the smallest of details. So, without further ado . . .'

Dan-Dan reaches up and presses a switch. The wall behind him explodes. I cry out – with my sensitive hearing it's as if someone has struck a large bell with a hammer by the side of my head – and turn away instinctively. When the worst of the pain passes and I look again, Dan-Dan has leapt through a gaping hole in the side of the cruiser.

'Son of a bitch!' I roar, darting after him. I get to the hole, almost jump, but pull up short, not willing to throw myself into the great unknown. Instead, once I have control of myself again, I study the river beneath me.

Dan-Dan has landed in the water and is swimming towards a speedboat moored nearby. I think about jumping after him, but he has too great a lead on me. Reaching the boat, he climbs into it, starts the engine, waves nonchalantly at me, then powers away along the Thames, heading west.

'James bloody Bond,' I snarl. Then I laugh with grudging admiration. I hate that child-killing monster, but I have to admit he knows how to make a cool getaway.

As I watch Dan-Dan disappear into the sunset (well, it's not long after midday, but he's earned a bit of poetic licence), another chunk of the hull blows outwards and Justin Bazini and Vicky Wedge throw themselves into the river and make for a speedboat of their own. Now that I look closely, I realise there are several more tied to the ship. The lords and ladies of the Board had obviously planned for an invasion like this. I bet they never told the guards about the secret escape hatches. They wouldn't have considered their underlings worth saving.

Turning my back on the hole, I send a silent promise after Dan-Dan and the others. *We'll meet again, my wretched* darlings, *and you won't get away from me so easily next time.*

Then, still wincing from the noise of the explosion, I retrace my steps and head back up the stairs to see what's going on and discover how the Angels found me.

TWENTY -ONE

I pass Master Zhang as I'm climbing the stairs. He's moving in the opposite direction, down into the hold. He pauses to study me and I bow to him politely.

'You have been in the wars,' he notes.

'They made me fight several times every day,' I tell him.

He grunts. 'The fact that you survived this long proves that you were concentrating during your lessons.' Then he pushes on. I allow myself a wry chuckle. Master Zhang isn't a man to go wild with compliments.

I make my weary way to the arena. It's all quiet on the upper deck now. I want to run up there, get out of this prison as soon as I can. But Dr Oystein is waiting for me in the old dining hall. Answers first, release later.

When I get to the arena, I see that the doctor isn't the only one waiting for me. All of the Angels from my room are present, Ashtat, Carl, Shane, Jakob. Rage and the twins have hung around. Plus there's one more addition, but this guy isn't so welcome.

'*Barnes!*' I bellow, charging towards him, fingers tightening, meaning to do all the things to him that I can't do to the departed Dan-Dan.

Carl and Shane slide together to block my path.

'Easy,' Carl says.

'He's on our side,' Shane says.

'Never,' I bark. 'He only looks out for himself.'

I try to push through. Carl and Shane shove me back. I get ready to fight.

'It's true, B,' Dr Oystein says softly. 'He came to us at County Hall, told us what was happening here, led us to you.'

I stop struggling. If I could, I'd blink like an owl.

Carl and Shane move apart. Barnes is standing directly ahead of me. He's taken the bullet from behind his ear and is tapping his front teeth with it. He raises an eyebrow when he spots my fingers clenching and unclenching.

'It's a real pisser when you don't know whether to thank a guy or spit in his eye, isn't it?' he smirks.

'I can't really spit these days,' I growl, 'but I'll never thank you either. What for—capturing me, enslaving me, bringing me here for Dan-Dan and the others to toy with?'

Barnes shrugs. 'As I told you before, our choices are sometimes limited. I have a son, Stuart, who means everything to me. He survived the attacks and was staying in a compound in the countryside. He was relatively safe there, but the compounds are no guarantee of long-term security. Several have fallen and others will too. When you're landlocked, you're always open to attack.

'I carried on hunting after my first run-in with you,' he continues. 'I made sure the zombies I killed weren't conscious, but otherwise it was business as normal. The members of the Board heard about me. They invited me to come visit. I was curious, so I paid them a call. They wanted to employ me to find new gladiators for them. But they weren't interested in ordinary zombies. They'd heard rumours that I'd met one who could talk.'

'How did they hear about that?' I sneer.

'I never discussed it with anyone,' Barnes said, 'but Coley and the others who were with us that day did. The stories intrigued the Board. They offered me a king's ransom to deliver you to them.'

'And you jumped at the chance.'

Barnes sniffs. 'I never cared about money. I couldn't be bought that way. But every man has his price. Mine was the safety of my son.' He sighs and sticks the bullet back behind his ear. 'They offered Stuart a place on one of the islands which are free of zombies. I tried getting him on to one of those before, but it's virtually impossible to gain access. Justin and his cronies operate several islands. If I agreed to work for them, they promised to ship out Stuart. I didn't even have to think about it.'

I glare at the hunter, still wanting to hate him, but finding myself thawing. If he's telling the truth, I understand. In his position I'd have done the same.

'So why the change of heart?' I scowl. 'Why play the hero now after serving the scumbags for so long?'

'The children,' Barnes says softly. 'I didn't know about them until they let me in here to watch you fight. A zombie's one thing, even a conscious one like you. But a live child ... As I said, my son means more to me than anything. But there are lines no man should ever allow himself to cross. I couldn't turn a blind eye to what Dan-Dan was doing to the children. As far as we've fallen, I don't ever want to fall that far.'

'We will do all that we can to safeguard your son's future,' Dr Oystein says. 'Zhang will scour every inch of this ship in search of the Board members. Two have already been dealt with. If the others are still alive, we will find them. They will not be able to harm your boy once we have dealt with them.'

'Be careful what you promise, doc,' I mutter. 'I killed Lord Luca but the others got away. They had escape hatches in the hull which they were able to blow open. There were speedboats moored to the cruiser. Justin, Vicky and Dan-Dan all made it to freedom.'

Barnes's face whitens. He starts to tremble, then stops himself. 'I have to go,' he tells Dr Oystein.

'You can stay with us if you wish,' Dr Oystein says. 'We can hunt for them together.'

Barnes shakes his head. 'I don't know where they'll go. But I know where my son is. I'll try to get to the island and rescue him before it occurs to them to order his execution. They might not even be aware of my treachery. They weren't on deck when we boarded. I might have time to play with.'

'I wish you luck,' the doctor says.

'Thanks.' Barnes grimaces. 'I'm going to need it.' The hunter faces me and tries to think of something to say. In the end he simply shrugs. 'Like I said to you once before, it won't mean anything, I'm sure, but I'm sorry.'

'Me too,' I mumble. 'By the way,' I stop him before he leaves, 'where's Coley?'

Barnes manages a weak grin. 'He never would have gone for this. He didn't care about the children. I knocked him out and tied him up before I went to County Hall. I'll swing by and free him before setting off for the island. It's the end of our partnership, but I owe him that much.'

'Was he the one you were talking about the last time you came to see me?' I ask. 'When you said it was hard having to sacrifice someone you care about?'

'No,' Barnes smiles, warmly this time. 'I was talking about *you*.'

As I stare at him, he flips me a quick salute, then hurries out of the arena and heads off to try and save the one person in the world he truly loves, the boy whose life he risked in order to do what was right.

Barnes did something heroic and noble today. But if his son is killed as a result, he'll feel like the most miserable man alive. Everyone knows this isn't a world of black and white, but it's not a world of grey either. It's a world of hellish, soul-tormenting red, and Barnes is adrift on that choppy, bloodstained sea the same as the rest of us. I hope the ex-soldier finds his son and enjoys a bit of peace before his number is called.

But I wouldn't bet on it.

TWENTY -TWO

'We should get you back home as soon as possible,' Dr Oystein says. 'You need to spend a few weeks in a Groove Tube.'

'I've been in there a lot recently,' I sigh. 'One mauling after another. I must be the most unfortunate girl in the world.'

'Some might think otherwise,' the doc murmurs. 'If you had not been captured and forced to fight, and if you had not determined the conditions under which you would compete, how many children would Daniel Wood have killed? Some might say you are a hero.'

I snort. 'A zombie can't be a hero. We're monsters.'

Dr Oystein smiles. 'Then all I can say is that I wish there were more monsters like you in the world.'

We beam at each other. Then I shake my head before things get too mawkish. 'So how did it go down? Barnes came to you, told you what was happening and led you here?'

'In a nutshell, yes. He spotted the twins while they were gathering supplies. He approached them, explained the situation and asked for their help. They escorted him back to County Hall.'

'That's why Dr Oystein let us come on this mission,' Cian says proudly. He looks like the cat that not only got the cream but a mouse-flavoured stick to stir it with. 'If not for us, Barnes might never have found his way to County Hall, certainly not in time to save you.'

'We begged the doctor and Master Zhang to let us tag along and they agreed in the end,' Awnya says.

'I wouldn't say that we *begged*,' Cian grumbles.

'Why are you guys soaked to the skin?' I ask.

'We were part of the river team,' Awnya says.

'Most of us were,' Carl adds.

Now that I look closely, I see that all of the Angels in the room are wet, except for Dr Oystein and Rage.

'We could not attack from land,' Ashtat explains. 'The guards on deck had the surrounding area covered. They would have torn us to pieces with their rifles before we could close the gap.'

'The doc and I came back with Barnes,' Rage says. 'He tied us up, loose knots that we could wriggle out of. Pretended to the guards that he'd captured us.'

'We came at a time when he knew the Board would be watching you fight,' Dr Oystein says. 'We hoped to swoop on them when they were together, for the sake of Barnes's son.'

'While the guards were ogling the doctor and Rage,' Carl says, 'the rest of us scaled the far side of the cruiser. We'd swum here earlier in the day and were waiting just beneath the surface of the water.'

'We plugged our ears and noses and kept our

mouths shut,' Cian says. 'Bobbed about there for more than an hour. It was cool!'

'I spotted a couple of speedboats while we were climbing,' Jakob says softly. 'I thought that was how the humans got to and from the ship. If I'd guessed they were for getaways, I would have torn holes in their hulls and sunk them.'

'How many of you came?' I ask.

'Most of the Angels,' Ashtat says.

'Every single Angel volunteered,' Shane says.

'I wasn't going to,' Rage sniffs, 'but I didn't want to be the odd one out. Would have looked bad.'

'You're all heart,' I grunt.

'We left some behind to take care of the place,' Carl says. 'Otherwise we're all here.'

'For *you*,' Dr Oystein whispers.

I shrug. 'What do you want me to do? Go round and thank everyone in person?'

'It wouldn't be a bad start,' Rage growls.

'Well, don't worry,' I laugh. 'I was planning to do just that. I might even hug a few of you beautiful buggers while I'm at it.'

'You see, B?' Dr Oystein says with a justified smile. 'You cannot be a true loner when you have so many people who love you.'

'*Love?*' I ask, arching an eyebrow at Rage.

Dr Oystein purses his lips. 'Well, maybe that is not *quite* the right word.'

'You don't have to hammer it home,' I tell him. 'I was wrong. I acted like an idiot. I'm sorry. I won't cut myself off from the rest of you again. I understand how lucky I am to have you guys on my side and I won't look to go it alone any more. Now, high-fives!'

And, like some overexcited kid after winning a cup final, I go around high-fiving everyone in the room, Dr Oystein, the twins, Carl, Jakob, Ashtat, Shane, even a cynically grinning Rage. And I don't feel the least bit embarrassed, because I'm not in the company of room-mates, colleagues or allies.

I'm with friends.

To be continued . . .

A NOTE FROM THE AUTHOR ON WRITING *ZOM-B GLADIATOR*

I wrote a brief plot outline for *Zom-B Gladiator* (although it was called Zom-B Gladiators at the time, as originally I meant to have other Angels involved in the action) on the 4th of August 2009, but it was the 6th of April 2010 before I started to flesh out the ideas and set to work on the book. I did my final edit of the book more than three years later, near the end of May 2013.

I was really looking forward to this book after the quieter, less action-packed double-hitter of *Zom-B Angels* and *Zom-B Baby*. Those books were essential to B's development and grounding the series, but it was nice to be able to throw in some truly gripping, dramatic fight scenes again! Plus I got to introduce a whole host of new villains for B to contend with, including one of my all-time favourites from any of my books – the despicable Dan-Dan!

Dan-Dan was actually named after my wife's nephew. His name is Daniel, but he was a young boy when I was writing this book, and everyone referred to him as Dan-Dan. It was such a lovely, sweet name that I thought it would be the perfect contrast for the disgusting child-killer in the book.

Since Dan-Dan wasn't the only villain in the book, I decided I'd use the names of more of my wife's family members for most of the other members of the Board. Justin Bazini is named after her brother (I tweaked the surname slightly – it's actually Basini). Vicky Wedge is named after his wife – she comes from the Wedgewood family, which is where the surname originated (while the Wood part of it became the surname of Dan-Dan and his brother). Lord Luca is named after my wife's other nephew, and Lady Jemima after her niece.

The Basinis are a lovely family in real life, and I've always enjoyed spending time with them. I hope they enjoy what I've done with them – they certainly seemed to like it when I read out an extract to them at Christmas, when the book was released!

The characters of Emma and Declan were also named after real people – my brother and his wife. I'd actually used Declan in a book before, in *The Saga of*

Darren Shan, but I figured there was enough distance between the two series for that not to be an issue.

I had to tread cautiously with Dan-Dan. He's a deliciously over-the-top villain, but because there's nothing fantastical about him, I had to be careful not to make him TOO disturbing. Fantasy allows you a lot of leeway as a writer – since Lord Loss was a creature from another dimension, i.e. a pure fantasy creation, I could have him ripping people to shreds, left, right and centre, and nobody minded, because he was clearly not real. But since genuine monsters like Dan-Dan do exist, he's far more unsettling than Lord Loss or Desmond Tiny, so I had to be careful not to push this into the realms of adult literature. To be fair to my editors, they let me go a long way with him, and only occasionally asked me to rein him in.

The HMS *Belfast* played an important role in this book. I visited the cruiser as a child, but haven't been back to it since. I meant to go back and do some research, but then I found plans and videos of it online, and I was able to use those instead. Some writers insist on experiencing everything that they write about in person – if they set a scene in a specific place, they go visit that place and write about what they find. But I love the internet and make as much use of it as I can. Sometimes it can be limiting, and then I have to get out into the field to do some research in the flesh, but I'm constantly amazed by just how much I can find out with a few Google searches and a bit of imagination.

We get to see just how far B has come as a character in *Zom-B Gladiator*. From being a shallow, selfish, borderline racist in book 1, she's now come to a point where she's prepared to risk her life every day, and go through all sorts of torments, in an attempt to help others. We also see how she's developed as a fighter – that training under Master Zhang really pays off here!

The book marks the end of the first half of the series – B's growth as a person – and that's why it's the only one of the twelve that doesn't end on a cliffhanger. I wanted readers to be able to pause at this point, reflect on what has gone before, and smile at B's accomplishments. The storyline moves forward quickly from book 7 onwards, and it's going to be an adrenaline rush from there until the end, with B facing all sorts of challenges and twists. As the old saying goes – you ain't seen nothing yet!!

Until then, take care – and watch out for Dan-Dan!